MAN OF ACTION

OMEGA SECTOR: CRITICAL RESPONSE

JANIE CROUCH

INTRIGUE

Edge-of-your-seat intrigue, fearless romance

AVAILABLE THIS MONTH

ISBN-13: 978-0-373-69917-9

EAN

He walked up to Andrea, careful to come at her slowly and from the side so he didn't sneak up on her in any way.

"Hi." He kept his voice even, calm. "What are you doing out here? Everything okay?"

She looked at him, then back at the parking lot.

Without being obvious about it, Brandon withdrew his weapon from the holster at his side. Had she seen something to do with the case?

"Andrea." His voice was a little stronger now. "What's going on? Is it something to do with the murders? Did you see something or did someone threaten you?"

She kept staring.

"Andrea, look at me."

She finally turned to him, hair plastered to her head from the rain, makeup beginning to smear on her face.

"I need you to tell me what's happening so I can do something about it."

MAN OF ACTION

—

JANIE CROUCH

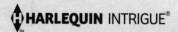

HARLEQUIN INTRIGUE®

To Anu-Riikka, because you talk me down from the ledge with
almost every single book. Thank you for listening to me for hours
on end and for offering a fresh perspective when I can't see clearly
any longer. You're the greatest buddy a writer could have.

ISBN-13: 978-0-373-69917-9

Recycling programs
for this product may
not exist in your area.

Man of Action

Copyright © 2016 by Janie Crouch

Printed in U.S.A.

www.Harlequin.com

Janie Crouch has loved to read romance her whole life. She cut her teeth on Harlequin Romance novels as a preteen, then moved on to a passion for romantic suspense as an adult. Janie lives with her husband and four children overseas. She enjoys traveling, long-distance running, movie watching, knitting and adventure/obstacle racing. You can find out more about her at janiecrouch.com.

Books by Author

Harlequin Intrigue

Omega Sector: Critical Response

Special Forces Savior
Fully Committed
Armored Attraction
Man of Action

Omega Sector

Infiltration
Countermeasures
Untraceable
Leverage

Primal Instinct

CAST OF CHARACTERS

Brandon Han—Omega Sector's most brilliant profiler. He holds doctorate degrees in both interpersonal communication and criminal justice, as well as being licensed to practice law. His specialty is being able to get inside the heads of killers, but the darkness inside his own mind sometimes threatens to overtake him.

Andrea Gordon—A naturally talented behavioral analyst who can read the body language and emotions of people around her to an astounding degree. She's desperate to hide her sordid past from the knowledge of her Omega Sector colleagues.

Steve Drackett—Director of the Critical Response Division of Omega Sector.

Grace Parker—Head psychologist of Omega Sector.

Lance Kendrick—A deputy of the Maricopa County sheriff's department in Andrea's hometown of Buckeye, Arizona.

Keira Spencer—A dear friend of Andrea's still working in Buckeye. She knows what Andrea has overcome in her life.

Jarrod McConnachie—A Buckeye local who knew Andrea in high school; he doesn't have a job and still lives with his mother.

DJ Shawn "Shocker" Sheppard—Local Phoenix DJ who takes pride in making his listeners squirm. His newest gimmick: the Angels & Devils Pilgrimage to strip clubs all over the state.

Harry Minkley—Owner of Jaguar's, Andrea's prior place of employment.

Prologue

Andrea Gordon huddled inside her car in the bank parking lot as pandemonium reigned all around her. Cops, SWAT, ambulances and other emergency vehicles she didn't even recognize flooded the area. Blue and red lights flashed in a rhythm that drummed brutally against her eyes. Officers pointed assault rifles toward the building. People ran back and forth.

Just behind the roped-off section, news crews formed the next layer of people, their lights and cords and equipment adding to the chaos.

Beyond that were the witnesses, the gawkers, hoping to catch something exciting. Andrea wasn't sure what would pacify them. A chase? Bullets? A dead body? Smartphones recorded the scene from every angle.

Three men had taken sixteen people hostage after an attempted robbery had gone wrong in a bank just outside Phoenix, Arizona. Andrea would've been one of those sixteen, but she had seen the signs on the robbers' faces when they'd first walked in.

Danger. Violence.

Andrea was only nineteen years old, but she was an expert at spotting the approach of danger. Maybe she should be thankful for all the times she'd had to discern it in her uncle to avoid his fists. Either way, it had gotten her out of that bank before the trouble went down.

The men hadn't come in together, but they were definitely working as a team; Andrea had immediately seen that. It was obvious to her that they weren't afraid to hurt, even to kill. Simmering violence was a vibe she was very attuned to.

Two of the men fairly buzzed with it. Excited about taking money that wasn't theirs and maybe taking a life, too. But it was the third man, who stood completely still and broadcast almost no outward emotions at all, that scared her the most.

She'd waited a minute longer, studying them while pretending to fill in a deposit slip, in case she was wrong. The two hyped-up guys were making their way back toward the bank manager's office. The other man, the scary one, stood against a side wall, a briefcase in his hand. He caressed it with a lover's touch.

He felt her eyes and turned to her, giving a smile so dark, so full of violence, Andrea had turned and nearly run out of the bank. She'd felt his eyes follow her as she left.

She'd been the last one out. Not two minutes after her exit, shots had been fired inside. The robbery soon turned into a hostage situation. Once out, Andrea had hidden in her car, parked in the back of the bank lot, and watched as the police arrived minutes later, then observers, then press.

Andrea would've been escorted back with the observers if anyone had known she was in her car. She'd been so scared at the third man's evil smile, she had literally melted herself into the driver's seat of her vehicle, curling into a ball and protecting her head and face with her arms.

She'd learned long ago that position didn't stop pain, but at least this time it had kept her away from anyone's view. The uniformed officer who had been in charge of security and taping off the parking lot had walked right by Andrea's car without even seeing her in the dimming hours of twilight.

Unfortunately, now she was trapped here since the lot was blocked off by police vehicles. There was no telling how long the showdown could continue with the three men inside. She would need to go find someone who could let her out if she wanted to leave this evening.

Andrea exited her car, kept her head down and walked toward the action, planning to talk to the first relatively nice cop she could find. She didn't want to draw any attention to herself, just wanted to get the help she needed and get out.

When she got to the front line of police officers, Andrea started looking around more. There was a lot of excitement in most of these cops. Some were nervous, a few downright fearful. A couple were bored.

She was easily able to spot the man in charge. He exuded self-confidence and self-importance, even without a radio in each hand and people constantly asking him questions. When he gave orders he expected them to be followed, and he was definitely the one giving orders in this situation. Another man and woman were standing with him. Everything about their faces and body language also suggested confidence, but they were respectful, caring—not power hungry. They stood back slightly, observing.

Drawn by the situation even though she didn't want to be, Andrea made her way toward those people in charge. She was careful not to get in anybody's way or do anything to draw someone's scrutiny, although she expected to be stopped at any moment. When she got close enough to hear the leaders, she stood beside an unmarked sedan, watching them studying and discussing the bank.

She heard the man and woman—the observers—arguing with the man in charge.

"Lionel, deadly force isn't necessary yet," the man stated, quiet but emphatic. "Plus we don't know the exact situation. We have no inside intel."

"This isn't your operation, Drackett," the man named Lionel snapped. He wasn't interested in anyone else's opinions. "Omega isn't in charge here—the Bureau is."

"We're not even sure how many perps are in there, nor how many hostages," the woman said, her voice as calm as Drackett's had been.

"We've got eyes on the building. There's obviously two gunmen holding a room of seventeen people. They've got everyone in one location to keep them in line."

Lionel was wrong. There were *three* men involved. But Andrea imagined the third one with the evil smile just looked like one of the hostages if he hadn't made any obvious threatening moves. With his briefcase and suit he'd blend right in.

And he meant to kill everyone in the building. Everything in his body language and his emotions had screamed violence.

"Neither of those guys have hurt anyone yet. Let us get our hostage negotiator down here to talk to them. Matarazzo is a whiz in this type of situation—you know that." Drackett again. "He can be here within the hour."

Lionel shook his head. "No, I don't need your rich wonder boy. I will handle this the way I see fit. The two gunmen have left the back of the building ripe for our entry. They are obviously camped in the front. They're nervous. I'm not going to wait until they kill someone before I make my move."

Although their expressions changed for only the briefest moment, Andrea could feel the waves of frustration coming off Drackett and the woman he was with. Whatever was going on, it was personal. Lionel all but hated Drackett.

That disdain was going to get everyone in the building killed. She could hear Lionel getting a SWAT team ready to breach the back door.

She was afraid when they did, the third man would make his move. She had to tell the police leaders what she knew. She didn't know if it would make a difference, if they would listen to her at all, but she had to try.

She walked over to Drackett and the woman before she could let herself chicken out. She didn't try to talk to Lionel; she already knew he wouldn't listen to her.

"Excuse me, Mr. Drackett? There's a third man inside that bank. Someone more deadly than the other two you can see."

Drackett immediately turned his focus to her, as did the woman. It was a little overwhelming. Andrea wasn't used to people actually listening to her that intently.

"How do you know?" His voice was clipped but she knew it was because they were running out of time, not because he didn't believe her.

"I was in there. I saw them come in. I'm—I'm pretty good at reading people, their expressions. I could tell something was not right with the three of them. Those two guys." She pointed at the bank doors where the two men could be seen. "And another one you don't know about."

Drackett and the woman met eyes and stepped closer to Andrea. She could tell they had Lionel's attention also, although he didn't turn toward them.

"I'm Grace. Tell us everything, as quickly as you can." The woman touched her on the arm. Andrea fought the urge to flinch even though she knew the woman meant her no harm.

"The two men, the ones with guns, are excited, a little shaky. They're thrilled about a big payoff and perhaps about having to shoot their way out of the situation. They will kill if they have to, but that's not their primary intent."

"And the third man?"

"Evil." Even in the Phoenix evening heat, Andrea felt cold permeate her bones. "He'll kill everyone. *Wants* to kill everyone. I think he wants to take as many people as possible down with him."

Drackett whispered something to Grace and she eased back and disappeared into the crowds of law enforcement. She was gone too quickly for Andrea to get a read on whether she believed Andrea or not.

"So help me God, Drackett, if you tell me we need to listen to what this child is telling us…"

"This young woman has more actual intel than anyone else here. I'm not asking you to stand down, Lionel, just to listen and make sure you have all the facts before making any big move."

"I'm not going to wait for these gunmen to kill someone before we move in. SWAT will be ready to storm the back door in three minutes. We go then."

Everything about Lionel screamed determination. Andrea didn't even try to convince him; he wasn't going to listen to her.

She took a step back. She had done all she could do. Things inside the bank would play out the way they would play out.

She was about to fade back even more when Drackett looked down at a message on his phone. He turned and walked the three steps so he was standing directly in front of her.

"You. Name. First and last."

"Andrea Gordon." He wasn't angry with her but the abrupt statement had her giving her real name rather than a fake.

"Just wanted to know the name of the person who's going to cost me my career if you're wrong," he whispered. "Go stand back there with that uniformed officer. All hell is about to break loose." He motioned for the officer to come get her.

Andrea walked back with the cop, but when he became distracted with something else, she slipped away. She eased into the crowds. She'd come back for her car another time.

She heard and felt the chaos behind her a few moments later. A shot fired then a bunch of people yelling. She just kept walking, not looking back.

ANDREA WASN'T SURE what had happened in the bank that evening. She'd watched the news the next day and it seemed as if the men had been stopped without any problems. One of the gunmen had been wounded in the raid; the other had surrendered without a fight. All the hostages had left the bank unharmed.

The third man was never mentioned or shown by the media. Andrea accepted that maybe she had been wrong; maybe he hadn't had anything to do with it. But then she thought of that evil smile the man had given her in the bank. Even now it had the ability to make her stomach turn.

Andrea hoped Mr. Drackett and Grace hadn't gotten in trouble because of what she had told them. She'd probably never have any way of knowing, so she put it out of her mind.

Until they both walked in to Jaguar's a couple of hours later.

Andrea was immediately self-conscious. She wasn't onstage dancing—thank God—but she was serving drinks, and even though the waitress outfits were more concealing than whatever the dancer was wearing, it still left very little to the imagination.

They were obviously here for her. Jaguar's rarely got customers in business suits. Especially suits that screamed law enforcement.

It was too dark for Andrea to read their expressions and body language as well as she would like, but anger radiated off them. This had to be about the bank. They must have gotten in trouble. And now they were here to let Andrea know. She wondered if she was about to be arrested.

"Harry, I need a break. I'll be back in fifteen," she said to her manager.

Harry leered at her the way he always did. "Any more than that and I'll dock your pay." He stepped closer, grasping her chin. "Or we can work out our own way of you paying me back."

He didn't see that Drackett and Grace had made their way up behind him, overhearing his words. Drackett cleared his throat.

Harry pegged them as cops as soon as he turned around. "And by paying me back, I mean working extra shifts," he muttered, going to stand farther behind the bar, glaring at the suits.

"Andrea, could we talk to you outside for a few minutes?" Grace said over the thump of the music.

"Am I about to be arrested?"

Drackett's eyes narrowed. "Why do you say that?"

Andrea shrugged, very aware of how much her clothes revealed. Her skimpy bra was clearly noticeable through the mesh of her top. The short pleated skirt she wore barely covered her bottom, and men often took it as an invitation to run their hand up her thigh.

Andrea had stopped slapping their hands away once Harry threatened to fire her.

She was used to men gawking at her body, but Mr. Drackett's eyes hadn't so much as left her face once since he'd arrived.

"You're angry," she said. It wasn't terribly noticeable in his expression, but she could tell.

Grace was surprised. "I don't think Steve is angry, Andrea." She turned to him. "Maybe we're wrong about her."

Steve shook his head once. "No, she's spot-on. I'm pissed as hell that she's working in a place like this." He stepped closer to Andrea and she couldn't help but take a step back. He froze. "I'm not angry at *you*, I promise."

Andrea believed him. "Okay."

"But do you mind coming outside with us? This will only take a few minutes."

Andrea grabbed her lightweight jacket and followed them out the side door. "I can't stay out here very long. I'll get fired if I do. I need this job," she said in the quieter, cooler air of outside. Finally she felt as if she could breathe again.

"You were right about the third man in the bank." Grace smiled at her. "You probably saved a lot of lives yesterday. He had a briefcase full of explosives and was just waiting to use them. Was waiting for SWAT so he could take them down, too."

Andrea closed her eyes in relief. At least no one had gotten hurt and these two people hadn't gotten fired.

"Andrea, I'm going to cut right to the chase." Mr. Drackett kept his distance so she wouldn't feel uncomfortable. "We believe you have a gift at reading people's emotions and microexpressions, even when they're only available for a split second."

Andrea wasn't exactly sure what microexpressions were, but she knew she was good at reading people.

"Maybe." She shrugged, clutching her jacket to her chest. "So?"

"I'm Steve Drackett. Grace and I work for Omega Sector: Critical Response Division. We're law enforcement, sort of like the FBI, but without as much red tape."

"And smarter and better looking," Grace chimed in, smiling again. "We're based out of Colorado Springs."

That was all fine and good, but what did it have to do with her? "Okay."

Drackett crossed his arms over his chest. "We'd like you to come work for us."

"What?" Andrea wasn't sure she was hearing right. "Doing what?"

"What you did at the bank. What you seem to be a natural at doing, if we're not mistaken. Reading people."

Andrea's gaze darted over to Grace then back to Drackett. "You don't even know me. Maybe I just got lucky at the bank."

Steve tilted his head to the side. "Maybe, but I don't think so. There are some tests that can help us know for sure. We'll pay for you to fly to Colorado Springs and for all your expenses during testing."

Andrea grimaced. Tests, books, schooling were not her strengths. The opposite, in fact. She looked down at her feet. "I'm not too good at tests. Didn't finish high school."

"It won't be like math or English tests you took in school," Grace said gently. "It's called 'behavioral and nonverbal communication diagnostic testing.'"

Now Andrea was even more confused. "I don't know what that means."

Grace smiled. "Don't worry about the name. The testing will involve a lot of pictures, or live people, and we'll see how accurately you can pick up their emotions and expressions."

Okay, only reading emotions, not words. Maybe she could handle it, but she still wasn't sure. What if she failed?

"Andrea!" Harry yelled from the door. "Time's up."

Steve looked at Harry then back to Andrea. "There are no strings in this offer," Steve said, his voice still calm and even. "You can check us out before you get on the plane, make sure we're legit. Read up about Omega, so you feel safe."

Andrea studied them both. There was no malice in either of them as they looked back at her, just respect, concern and a hopefulness. They legitimately seemed to want her to join them.

"What if I can't do what you want? If I'm not as good as you think?" she whispered.

"Then you'll be paid handsomely for the time you've spent doing the testing," Grace said. "And we'll fly you anywhere you want to go. It doesn't have to be in Arizona."

"Andrea." Harry's voice was even louder. "Get your ass back in here. Now."

"And we'll help get you started in another career. It may not be with Omega, but it doesn't have to be here. This is not the place for you. Why don't you leave with us tonight?" The compassion in Steve's face was her undoing.

She looked back at Harry. He was livid, wanted to hurt her physically, emotionally, any way he could. It seemed as if there had been someone wanting to hurt her all her life.

But Steve and Grace didn't. They wanted to help. She just hoped she didn't disappoint them.

Andrea slipped her jacket all the way onto her body. "Okay, I'll come with you."

There was nothing worth keeping her here.

Chapter One

Four years later, Andrea stood in front of a bathroom mirror inside Omega Sector headquarters. She smoothed her straight black skirt and made sure—again—that her blouse was tucked in neatly before checking her reflection in the bathroom mirror one last time. Blond hair, cut in a sleek bob—the most professional haircut she'd been able to think of—was perfectly in place. Makeup tastefully applied and nothing that would draw attention to herself.

She was about to be fired from her job as a behavioral analyst at Omega Sector's Critical Response Division.

Why else would Steve Drackett be calling her into his office at ten thirty on a Monday morning?

Actually, she could think of a half dozen reasons why he would be calling her in: a new case, a new test, some assignment he needed her to work on or a video briefing where her analysis was needed. But her brain wasn't interested in focusing on any of the logical reasons he wanted to meet with her.

"Steve and Grace both know your background and still want you here," she told her reflection. The scared look didn't leave her eyes. She forced herself to vacate the bathroom and head down the hall. If Steve was going to fire her, there was nothing she could do about it.

No one said hello to her as she walked through the corridors and Andrea didn't engage anyone. She'd utilized this keep-to-herself plan ever since she had realized exactly how important Omega was and the caliber of people they had working here in the Critical Response Division. Ever since Steve and Grace had officially offered her a job four years ago after six weeks of testing.

She may have a gift of reading people, but Andrea didn't think for one minute that she was the sort of person Omega normally hired.

She'd known from the beginning she needed to keep her past a secret. Announcing to her colleagues that she was a runaway, dyslexic high school dropout who—oh yeah—*used to be an exotic dancer* would not inspire much confidence in her. So she'd made it a point not to tell anyone. Not to ever discuss her past or personal life at all. If it didn't involve a case, Andrea didn't talk about it.

Her plan hadn't won her any friends, but it had successfully worked at keeping her secrets. She could live without friends.

Andrea pushed on the door that led to the outer realm where Steve's assistants worked. One of them stood, welcoming and walking her to Steve's office door and opening it. The clicks of Andrea's three-inch heels on the tiled floor sounded more like clanging chimes of doom in her head as she stepped through.

"Hey, Andrea, good to see you," Steve said from behind his desk, looking up from a stack of papers.

She supposed he was handsome, with his brown hair graying slightly at the temples and his sharp blue eyes, but since he was nearly twenty years older than her, she'd never even thought of him in that way. She respected him with every fiber of her being. Not only for getting her out of a dead-end life back at Jaguar's in Buckeye, Arizona, but because of how fair and respectful he acted toward all the people who worked at Omega.

But he was tired. Andrea could tell. "You need a vacation, boss. Some time away from this circus."

Steve put his elbows on his desk and bridged his fingers together, grimacing just the slightest bit. "You know why I don't invite you in here very often? Because you see too much." But his words held no fire. He knew what she said was right.

Andrea nodded.

"Sit down, Andrea. I'm afraid what I have to say might be a little difficult to hear."

Oh my God, he is *going to fire me.*

Andrea took a breath through her nose and tried not to let her panic show. She had known this was a possibility from the beginning. Not just a possibility, a *probability*.

She tried to mentally regroup. Okay, she wasn't the same girl who had left with Steve and Grace from Buckeye. She had managed to successfully complete her high school equivalency degree and even had two years of college under her belt. Yes, her dyslexia made some classes difficult, and she had to take them at a slower pace than most people, but she was making progress.

She could get some other job now. She had money in savings. She didn't have to go back to Jaguar's and let those people paw at her again.

"Andrea."

Steve's tone made her realize it wasn't the first time he'd said her name. She finally forced herself to focus on what he was saying.

"I don't need to have your gift to see that you're panicking. What the hell is going on in that brain of yours?" She could feel waves of concern flowing from him, and it was easily readable on his face.

She rubbed her skirt again. "Steve, I understand if you need to let me go. I've always known that was a possibility—"

"Andrea, I'm not firing you."

"But you said this may be difficult."

"And it probably will be, but why don't you let me finish before you jump to conclusions."

Now Andrea felt the reprimand. She sank back a little in her chair. "Yes, sir."

"I need you for a case."

He really wasn't firing her. "Okay."

"It involves a serial killer. He's been striking in the Phoenix area, with the last woman found dead just outside of Buckeye."

Her hometown. Now his concern made sense.

"And you want me to go there." It wasn't a question.

"I think your ability as a behavioral analyst, plus your knowledge of and history with the area, makes you one of our best chances of stopping this guy as quickly as possible."

She was glad she wasn't being fired, but Steve was right—this was hard. She didn't want to go back to Buckeye. When she'd left there that night with Steve and Grace, she'd never returned. She'd gone back inside Jaguar's to collect her personal belongings and her tips and had told Harry she wasn't coming back.

She'd been glad to have Grace, obviously a cop and obviously carrying a weapon, standing behind her as she did it, because she didn't think Harry would've taken it so well otherwise. As it was, his face had turned a molten red, small eyes narrowed even further. But he hadn't stopped her.

She'd never really explained it all to Steve, but Jaguar's was really just the tip of her iceberg of bad memories when it came to Buckeye. The situation she'd lived through the years before she'd run away from her aunt and uncle's home had been much worse. She still bore a few scars to prove that.

"I know this is hard for you." Steve was studying her carefully from behind his desk.

"Buckeye is not somewhere I'd choose to visit." The understatement of the century.

Steve came around to sit on his desk, closer to her. "Andrea, you're not the same person Grace and I met in Buckeye four years ago. You're stronger, more confident, able to handle the stress of this job, which isn't a light matter."

"Yeah, but—"

"I know you feel like you don't have the same educational background or experience of most of the people actively working cases at Omega. But you have a natural talent at reading people that continues to be honed."

"But—"

Steve wasn't really interested in her arguments. "I can think of a dozen cases, just off the top of my head, where your assistance provided the primary components needed to allow us to make an arrest."

Andrea took a breath. She knew that. Intellectually, she knew all that Steve spoke was the truth. But it was so hard.

"You've got to stop thinking I'm about to fire you every time I call you to my office. I'm not, trust me. I can't afford to lose such a valuable member of the Omega team."

Steve radiated sincerity. Of course, he always had. And she did believe she was part of the team. A noneducated, ex-stripper part of the team, but part of the team.

Okay, she could handle this. She could handle going back to Buckeye.

"Of course, we won't be sending you alone. You and Brandon Han will be working together."

Andrea smiled through gritted teeth, glad that Steve wasn't as skilled at reading people as she was. Brandon Han, as in *Dr.* Brandon Han, with something like two PhDs and an IQ higher than Einstein. They called him "the machine." He was considered the best and most brilliant profiler at Omega.

Not to mention he was hotter than sin. Tall, black hair, with a prominent Asian heritage.

"Do you know Brandon?"

Besides when she'd fantasized about him? "Um, I've never worked any cases with him, but I've met him a couple of times, briefly."

She wasn't sure he would even remember meeting her.

"Great. He'll be here any minute. Then we can go over details and get you guys going today."

BRANDON HAN WAS running a little late for his meeting with Steve but knew his boss would understand. Brandon had just come from visiting the widow and kids of his ex-partner.

Brandon didn't get by to see them as much as he liked, but he knew there were other Omega people checking in on them, also. David Vickars had been a well-liked and respected member of the team. He'd had the backs of many agents over the years, and the Omega family didn't forget their own.

David had died a year ago from a foe even Omega couldn't fight: cancer. He'd worked active duty until a month before he died from an inoperable tumor, then spent his last weeks with his wife and kids.

Brandon and David had been partners for seven years and had been friends for long before that. Brandon hadn't been interested in working with a partner since David died.

But he knew the minute he walked into Steve Drackett's office and saw beautiful, blonde Andrea Gordon sitting in a chair, body language screaming nervousness, that he was about to get partnered again.

Damn it.

Brandon had become quite adept at working alone. He liked the quiet. He liked being able to work at his own pace, which—no conceit intended—was often quite a bit faster than everyone else's.

"Hey, Steve," he greeted his boss. He nodded at Andrea, but she'd looked away. Par for the course for her. She'd looked away every time he'd ever been in the same room with her.

Drackett stood from behind his desk and shook Brandon's hand. "Let's go over to the conference table to talk about a case."

Steve was moving them to neutral ground, not wanting to pull rank from behind his desk if he didn't have to. He wanted Brandon to agree to whatever was about to be asked without having to force him. If Brandon wasn't mistaken, his boss's friendliness had to do with Andrea. A protectiveness maybe.

"Sure," Brandon agreed amicably. He might as well let this play out.

Andrea stood and joined them. Brandon held out a chair for her, waiting to see if she was one of those women who got offended by the gesture. That would tell him a lot about her.

But she just looked surprised for a moment before taking the chair he held out. He helped slide it in as she sat.

Okay, not afraid of her own femininity and didn't feel that every situation needed to be a struggle of power.

"You've met Andrea Gordon?" Steve asked, glancing at them.

"Yes, a couple of times. Good to see you again."

"Yes, you too," she murmured, voice soft. Sweet, even.

"We've got a serial killer working in the Phoenix area. Three dead so far." Steve handed them both a file.

"Confirmed serial?" Brandon asked, glancing through the file.

"Pretty much as confirmed as these things can get. All three were women in their early twenties. All were found covered in some sort of white cloth and holding a lotus flower."

"Purity," Andrea muttered.

"What?" Steve asked.

Andrea shrugged. "Lotus flowers are the symbol of purity in some cultures."

"She's right," Brandon said. "And so is the white cloth. Almost like a cleansing ritual."

"Okay, that's something to go on. I'll need you two to leave tonight. The local police department is expecting you."

"Steve, since David…" *Died.* Brandon found it difficult to say the word even now a year later, so he just didn't. "Since David, I've been working alone. That's been going pretty well for me. I think I'm more productive that way."

Brandon turned to Andrea. "I mean that as no offense to you whatsoever."

Some emotion passed across her face but was gone before he—even with all his training—could read it. Frustrating.

"I understand," she said, nodding.

"Brandon, the last murder took place inside the town

limits of Buckeye, on the outskirts of Phoenix. That's where Andrea is from. With ritual killings like this, we both know it's usually someone from the area."

Brandon grimaced. He couldn't deny that. Having someone familiar with the area—especially someone with a stellar skill set like Andrea's—would be invaluable.

But still, Brandon didn't want to work with her. Didn't want to be in forced proximity with her for an extended length of time. He glanced over at her but she wasn't looking at him, again. She was studying the pictures in the file, as if she couldn't care less about the conversation going on around her.

Brandon's eyes narrowed. No, he did not want to partner with this woman for a case. He'd discovered over the past year that he liked working alone, but it was more than that.

He didn't trust Andrea. The woman had secrets. Secrets tended to blow up in everyone's faces at the most inopportune moments.

David had kept his illness a secret from everyone for as long as he could. Brandon didn't want to be around secrets anymore.

He especially didn't want to be around a stunningly beautiful woman with secrets. The kind of woman who made him want to toss out his never-mix-business-with-pleasure rule. The kind that made him want to find out all her secrets.

He didn't trust her and she was distracting. She damn well had distracted him every time he'd seen her the past few months. Including today. Her perfect legs in her perfect suit with her perfect hair and makeup. It all distracted him.

He was not a man who liked to be distracted.

Brandon could kill a man a dozen ways with his bare hands, but it wasn't his strength or speed he relied on to get ahead of criminals. He relied on his intellect, his education, his experience to stop the worst of the worst bad guys.

Having Andrea Gordon's distracting presence around him during a serial-killer case was just not going to work.

He leaned back in his chair and feigned a casualness he didn't have. "I just think it's better for me to work alone on this case."

Because he wasn't sure he'd be able to work at all otherwise.

Chapter Two

"She has secrets, Steve. Something she's not telling people."

Steve had already excused Andrea from his office and had told her—much to Brandon's vexation—to go pack for the trip to Buckeye.

"We all have secrets." Steve had moved himself back behind his desk. Evidently time for neutral ground was over. Steve was reaffirming that he was in charge.

"Do you know what they call her around here?"

Steve raised one eyebrow.

"'The ice queen.' She never talks to anyone, never engages anyone. Nobody knows anything about her."

"Just because she's not the life of the party makes her an ice queen? I thought better of you, Han."

Brandon didn't know why he felt the need to so quickly defend himself, but he did. "Not me. I didn't say that or think it, nor any of our inner group. It's just what I've heard some other people say."

"She's damn good at what she does. Next time someone wants to talk trash about her because she's not all touchy-feely, you be sure to tell them that."

"We all know she's good. She's a natural reader.

I've never seen anything like it." Brandon held a PhD in interpersonal communication and still couldn't read people's expressions and body language to the extent Andrea could.

"But?"

"No buts about that. All I'm saying is she has secrets."

"She has a past, Brandon. We all do. Hers is a little more bleak than most of ours. If she's got secrets it's because she wants to not live in that past."

Brandon had to admit there was nothing wrong with that.

"I know it hurt you when David didn't tell you about his cancer. To find out then lose him so quickly was tough. It was for all of us."

Brandon got up out of his chair and walked over to the window. "I want to say this isn't about David, but of course that's not true."

"I know he was your best friend too, Brandon."

Brandon nodded without turning around. David had been his best friend since long before they worked together at Omega. David had been his anchor when the darkness of wandering inside the minds of killers had become too much.

"Andrea's the top person for this case, just like you're the top person for this case. There's somebody out there murdering young women and he needs to be stopped before he kills again."

Brandon knew Steve was right.

"Andrea's young, only twenty-three," Steve continued. "She's unsure about her abilities and where she fits in here."

Twenty-three? Something inside Brandon eased. She *was* young. Brandon was only thirty-one, but twenty-three seemed like a lifetime ago. He'd been more unsure about himself then too, so he couldn't blame her.

"You know me, Steve. I like having all the facts going into anything. She's an unknown variable and it gets my hackles up."

"I know some of what she keeps to herself, and although I am not at liberty to share, what I know about her makes me respect her more, not less. But some of her secrets she's never shared with me. May not have shared them with anyone. That's her choice."

Brandon nodded. As Steve said, everyone had secrets.

"She's damn good at her job and she'll help you find that killer."

Brandon ran a hand over his face. "Okay, you're right. I'll go pack."

"Han, thank you," Steve said as Brandon turned for the door. "I know this isn't easy."

"Like you said, the important thing is getting the killer off the street."

"Going back to that town is not going to be easy for her. I'd appreciate if you'd just keep an eye out for her emotional well-being."

"Anything in particular I should know about?"

Steve shrugged. "It's where she grew up. Faster than most, I would venture."

Somehow Brandon got the feeling there was a huge

chunk of information Steve was leaving out, but he let it slide. "Okay, I'll keep an eye out for her as best I can. Is that it?"

"Actually, no."

Brandon didn't even try to refrain from rolling his eyes. "There's more?"

"It's probably nothing, but I wanted to make you aware of it." Steve's tone had turned from concerned to downright serious.

Brandon walked back toward his desk. "Okay."

"Damian Freihof escaped from federal custody thirty-six hours ago."

Brandon filtered his mind for the information, finding it. "He was the guy who planned to blow up those people in that bank in Phoenix, right? What, three years ago?"

"Four. We also think he was responsible for two other bombings, but we weren't able to prove it."

"Do you suspect he's in Buckeye?"

"No. But like you said, the bank he tried to blow up was in Phoenix, pretty close by. He blames Andrea for his arrest."

"Why? Was she even there?"

"She was there, and she was the one who led to his capture, although she was not in law enforcement at the time."

Yeah, because at the time she would've been nineteen years old, if Brandon's math was correct.

"Did you tell Andrea about his escape?"

Steve's hesitation was minuscule, fleeting. Brandon would've missed it if he hadn't been trained to see it.

"No, we chose not to tell her. When Freihof went to prison, Andrea was not yet working for us. Plus with two life sentences we didn't figure he would be getting out until he was at least eighty. He escaped during a transfer."

"You think keeping her out of the loop is wise?"

Steve shrugged. "Freihof was mad at pretty much everyone during his case and sentencing, so we didn't—and still don't—give his threats against Andrea much credence. We're not even sure how he got Andrea's name since she wasn't involved in his arrest or trial, but I doubt he's after her now. All she really did was let us know there was a third man in the bank. I don't think she had any idea he planned to blow everyone up and that her info thwarted his attempt."

Another secret. Another potential problem.

"All right." Brandon nodded. "I'll keep my eyes peeled for any extra psychos while we're chasing down our current one."

Steve smiled. "Remember, she's not an agent, just a full-time consultant. She has some physical training, but not nearly as much as you do."

"Okay. I'll keep that in mind."

Steve shook Brandon's hand. "Good hunting. Keep me posted."

Brandon nodded and headed toward the door. This was already more complicated than Brandon liked it. And he knew it was just going to get worse.

BRANDON'S ARRIVAL AT the Colorado Springs Airport three hours later to discover the flight to Phoenix had been delayed due to mechanical issues did not make him feel any better about the start of this case. They were flying commercial since the two Omega jets were occupied with other missions.

Andrea showed up, still looking chic and cool in her skirt and blouse. The ice queen. Brandon wondered if she ever let herself get rumpled. His fingers literally itched with the desire to be the one who did it.

Rumpling Andrea Gordon was such a bad idea.

Brandon had noticed her around Omega for years—it was difficult not to notice someone who looked like Andrea—but he'd been very careful not to allow himself to study her. Not to try to figure out what made her tick and what made her smile or frown. With two advanced degrees in human behavior and communication, not to mention one in law, figuring people out was what Brandon did.

But with Andrea that had seemed a dangerous path to start down.

Then for the past year he'd been so involved in his own issues—David's death, learning how to work alone—that his attraction for Andrea had gotten pushed to the back burner. But now it was sitting down next to him in the airport chair, unavoidable.

"Hello." She smiled briefly at him. "Ready for this?"

Andrea wanted to be professional. Everything about her suggested it, from her prim clothes, to her tasteful makeup, to her perfect hair. Brandon would answer in kind. Professional was better for both of them.

He nodded. "Not quite up to speed yet, but getting there. We're scheduled to meet with the Phoenix and Buckeye police tomorrow. Evidently Buckeye's department isn't equipped to handle a homicide investigation, so Phoenix is helping out."

"Buckeye is small. They don't get many serial killers."

"Let's hope we can stop this one before he kills again."

He found her studying him as he took some files out of his briefcase, her expression a little bemused. "What?"

"Nothing." She shook her head. "You're just…complicated."

Brandon's eyes narrowed. Quite the interesting observation. "Why do you say that?"

She shrugged. "Most people only have one or maybe two main emotions transpiring inside them at the same time. You have more." Her lips pursed. "And they're complex."

He did have more. Brandon knew that about himself. Knew that he compartmentalized in order to be able to get more done, to think about different things without actually dwelling on them.

It was part of what made him a good profiler. His subconscious brain was able to continue to work on certain aspects of a case while his conscious brain focused on something entirely different. Part of it was his own natural ability and intelligence. Part of it came from years of training his brain to do what he wanted.

He also had darkness in him. He could admit that, too. A side of him that knew he could use his intellect and training and experience to commit crimes if he really wanted. And would probably never get caught.

It was never too far from the surface, although he never shared it with anyone.

Brandon had never had someone—especially someone who didn't really know him well—sense the complexity of the emotions inside him. It was disconcerting, particularly because he didn't want her to be able to read him so well.

"Oh." Andrea looked away from him.

"What?"

"Annoyance just swamped out pretty much everything else." She folded her hands in her lap and looked at them.

She thought he was annoyed with her, when really his annoyance stemmed from not having as much control over expressing his emotions as he thought he had. That was the problem with naturals, with people who were just gifted behavioral analysts rather than those who had studied human psychology and nonverbal communication to become experts. The naturals could read the emotions but couldn't always figure out the context.

"Let's just focus on the case, okay?" He handed her a bundle of files. "We pretty much need to be completely familiar with all of this before we meet with the locals tomorrow."

Andrea grimaced. "Okay."

So she didn't like to do her homework. She wouldn't get far solving cases without it. No amount of skill reading people could offset having a good understanding of the particulars of a case.

Brandon began reading through the files. He often found that insight came after the third or fourth read-through, rarely the first.

It didn't take him long to realize Andrea wasn't reading. She was looking at the photographs—the postmortem shots of the women as well as the crime-scene photos—but not actually reading any of the information that went along with them.

When she slipped on headphones and began listening to music or whatever, Brandon felt his irritation grow. Did she need a sound track to make it more interesting? Was death not enough?

Brandon knew different people processed information different ways. Some of his best friends at Omega often got insight on a case while in a workout room or in the middle of hand-to-hand sparring with someone. He should cut Andrea some slack. If she wanted to listen to music and just study the pictures, that was her prerogative.

But damn if it didn't piss him off. It didn't happen often, but she had fooled him. Who would've guessed that under the professional clothes and standoffish attitude rested the heart of a slacker. Brandon took a deep breath and centered himself. It wasn't his fault or his problem if she lacked motivation and self-discipline.

He'd told Steve he preferred to work alone. It looked as if, despite Andrea's attractive packaging, he'd be getting his wish.

Chapter Three

This whole thing was a terrible idea. Going back to Buckeye? Terrible. Going back with the likes of Brandon Han? Even worse. The plane hit some turbulence at thirty-five thousand feet, as if nodding in agreement with Andrea's conclusion.

Brandon didn't want to work with her on the case. He'd made that abundantly clear in Steve's office. She wanted to assume it was her fault, that he knew about her shortcomings and lack of education as an Omega consultant, but forced herself to stop. He'd mentioned liking to work alone. She could understand that, too. Andrea liked working alone, but for different reasons.

Brandon's irritation had been pretty tangible when she'd sat down next to him at the airport. It had just grown as they waited for their flight, first when she'd mentioned him being complicated, then when they were both looking through the case files.

By the time they got on the plane, about an hour after their scheduled departure time, Brandon was hardly even talking to her. He was mad—she had no idea why—and she was awkward—as usual around someone she was so attracted to. Good times.

Andrea tried to pretend she was reading the files when he handed them to her, but she wasn't. She knew better than to even try. Her dyslexia made reading simple books difficult, although she had learned some exercises to help with that. But reading handwritten notes and case files often written in different fonts and sizes—that pretty much just led to a headache and frustration.

She'd had an extra hour at her apartment, so she'd used the special software on her computer to scan a few pages so they could be converted into audio clips. She'd found that listening worked much better for her than trying to read. Unfortunately, she hadn't had enough time to scan all the files as she normally would.

Listening to the files on audio clips had just made Brandon more irritated. Andrea had no idea what to do about that, so she ignored it. She would listen to the clips she had, then spend this evening—all night if she had to—reading through the files in her room, when she was alone and it was quiet. She refused to go into that meeting with the local police tomorrow unprepared.

She didn't want to go back there at all. If it wasn't for Steve asking her to go, Andrea wouldn't have done it, serial killer or not.

Maybe they wouldn't run into anyone she knew. Or maybe the people in Buckeye wouldn't recognize her. She'd gone to great lengths to look nothing like the girl who had worked at Jaguar's. Her blond hair was shorter, cut in a flattering bob; her makeup was tasteful. She'd learned how to dress and present herself in a professional manner.

She doubted her own aunt and uncle would recognize her. Not that she planned to drop in on them. She hadn't seen them since the last time her uncle, in a drunken stupor again, had awakened her with a backhand that had sent her sprawling from her bed to the floor when she was seventeen. Another punch had sent her hurling into a glass table. She'd gotten away from him and hidden that night, wrapping her cut arm in a T-shirt.

The next morning she'd told her aunt, who'd looked the other way *again* during all the commotion, that she was going to school.

Andrea hadn't gone to school. And she hadn't gone back home. Ever again.

She hadn't gone far, just to the other side of the town she'd only ever known as home, but they hadn't come looking for her. Had probably been relieved that she'd left.

So yeah, no joyous homecoming in Buckeye.

Andrea withdrew into herself as they landed at Sky Harbor Airport. She let Brandon take the lead as they rented a car and headed west on I-10 out of Phoenix, stopping to get something to eat on the way. The stark, flat lands of Arizona were a huge contrast to the backdrop of the Rocky Mountains in Colorado Springs, where she'd spent the past four years.

Coming here was a mistake. Andrea was convinced of it. If she'd been alone, she might have turned around and gone back home.

Home, Colorado Springs. That was her home now.

"Hey, you doing okay?"

Andrea struggled to hide her shock at Brandon's

hand on her arm. She didn't think he was going to engage with her for the rest of the trip.

"Yeah. I just… This is hard. I don't think I want to do this."

She could feel his annoyance or coolness, or whatever it was he felt toward her, ease.

"Going back to the place where you grew up can be hard. Is there anyone you'd like to see while you're there? Friends? Family?"

"No, I don't think so. I don't think anyone here will remember me."

He didn't push it and she was thankful. They drove on in silence from the airport west on I-10 before turning south on smaller Highway 85. A couple of miles down they passed her old high school, Buckeye Union. Before thinking it through, she pointed it out to Brandon.

"What year did you graduate?"

She didn't want to tell him that she hadn't graduated, so she told him the year she'd stopped going. Then she realized it might make it sound as if she'd graduated early or something, so she changed it to the next year.

Brandon looked at her with one eyebrow raised, but fortunately, he didn't say anything else about it.

Before she knew it, before she could *stop* it, they were in Buckeye. The town hadn't changed much. They passed the dollar store, one of the town's grocery stores and Buckeye Auto Repair.

She actually remembered Buckeye Auto Repair pretty fondly. They had quite politely not mentioned that it looked as though everything she'd owned was in her car when she'd had to take it in for repairs when she was seventeen.

That was because everything she'd owned *had* been in the car. She'd been living in it at the time. Before she got the job at Jaguar's and made enough money to move into a sparsely furnished, run-down studio apartment.

She was pretty sure the owner of Buckeye Auto Repair hadn't charged her the full price for the repair.

She and Brandon pulled up to the town's one decent hotel. There were a couple of others on the rougher side of town—ones that were rented out by the hour, or the opposite, used to house multiple illegal immigrants in one room. This was a much better choice for law enforcement.

Brandon checked them in, getting rooms right next to each other on the first floor. They grabbed their bags and headed through the lobby and down the hall.

"I'm going to call it a night," Andrea said, slipping the key card into her door. She needed to be alone, away from all her thoughts and feelings about this town. She also needed to begin the painful process of studying the case files before tomorrow's meeting.

"Okay, I'll see you tomorrow. We'll leave at eight o'clock." Brandon turned to his door. "Are you okay?"

Andrea nodded. "Good night." She shut the door behind her without another word, away from Brandon and his brown eyes that saw too much.

Because she wasn't all right. Being back here was worse than she'd thought it would be.

This whole thing was a terrible idea.

THE NEXT MORNING at the Maricopa County Sheriff's Department office, Brandon and Andrea waited in the conference room for the local officers who would serve as their liaisons. The sheriff's department was just a mile or so on the outskirts of Buckeye.

When Andrea had seen what building they were arriving at, her eyes had nearly bugged out of her head. Her skin had turned a concerning shade of gray. Brandon had reached for her hand, and she had clutched his, almost automatically. Her skin was cold, clammy.

A sure nonverbal tell of fright. This building frightened Andrea.

She'd taken a couple of deep breaths and gotten herself under control, releasing his hand. She'd smiled over at him, an expression nowhere near touching her eyes, so nowhere near real. Something about that fake smile nearly broke his heart.

Maybe the whole idea of bringing her back to Buckeye had been a mistake. Her input would be valuable, sure, but Brandon had solved a lot of cases without having an inside person.

Maybe the price of doing this was too high for Andrea.

Whatever judgments Brandon had made about her began to dissipate a little. Maybe she just wasn't ready to deal with this.

"Andrea." He'd turned to her from where they sat in the parking lot. "Perhaps this isn't a good idea. It's okay if I need to go in alone."

"No, I'm fine. I just didn't realize we'd be coming *here*, to this building, that's all."

What was here that made her so upset? "You have some history here?"

She took a deep breath. "Not really. This whole town just sets me on edge."

"Are you sure you're okay?" He didn't want her to get inside then panic.

"Yes, I'm fine. I promise." The smile she gave him was at least a little stronger than the shadow of one she'd given him a few moments ago. He touched her hand. It was closer to normal temperature again.

But she looked tired, despite makeup that carefully covered it, as if she had been up most of the night. Maybe she had if the town had this sort of effect on her.

But except for the telltale signs that he was sure only he would notice, looking at her from across the conference table now, she looked like the consummate professional. Andrea wore sharp trousers and a matching blazer, managing to be attractively feminine and coolly businesslike at the same time. The high heels she wore everywhere were the perfect complement to the outfit. Not a hair was out of place in her chic bob.

She may have been scared out in the parking lot, but she was determined not to show it in here. Brandon's respect for her ratcheted a notch. If only she was as prepared for the case as she looked, which he knew she wasn't. Maybe he could help her out if she got stuck, save her any embarrassment.

Two men entered the room, one in his midfifties in a sheriff's office uniform, one in his early thirties in a suit. Both looked a little tired, frazzled. The older man took the lead. "I'm Lance Kendrick from the Maricopa County Sheriff's Department. Since all three murders took place—or at least the bodies were found—in Maricopa, I'm taking the lead."

"I'm Gerardo Jennison with the City of Phoenix Homicide Unit. We're providing investigative resources for anything which the sheriff's department may not have."

"I'm agent Brandon Han from Omega Sector, as you know. This is Ms. Andrea Gordon, one of our behavioral analysts. She'll be consulting as needed."

As Jennison shook Andrea's hand, Brandon could see his appreciation of her as a woman. Lance Kendrick, on the other hand, studied her pretty intently. Andrea had looked at him when they shook hands, but then glanced away.

Andrea recognized Kendrick.

That wasn't impossible or even improbable. Andrea had lived here her whole life. She probably would've run into members of the sheriff's office from time to time. "Have we met before?" Kendrick asked Andrea.

Her expression remained smooth although she shifted just slightly in her chair. "Maybe." She smiled at him. "Omega works a lot of cases."

A very nice side step. She wasn't offering up that she used to live here or that she recognized Kendrick, so Brandon didn't, either. Her comment seemed to pacify the sheriff's deputy, although Brandon knew that wasn't where they knew each other.

"We have three victims so far," Kendrick said, tone bordering on bored. "All Caucasian females between the ages of twenty to twenty-five. Cause of death was strangulation with a thin rope. The ligature marks were quite clear. All had been restrained—marks on their wrists were obvious, but there was no sign of any other assault, sexual or otherwise. And they all were found outside a church. Different one each time."

Putting the victims outside a church corresponded

well with the purity theme he and Andrea had batted around yesterday.

"Any known connection between the victims?" he asked.

"They didn't seem to know each other, as far as we can tell. All lived in Maricopa County, but different parts."

"But two had been arrested for something in the last year or two," Andrea interjected.

Brandon glanced at her discreetly. So she *had* studied the files.

Kendrick nodded. "Different charges, but yes. Brought here for holding, actually. One was arrested for solicitation, one for underage drinking. Neither of them were ever booked or went to trial."

If Brandon hadn't been looking over at Andrea, he would've missed her slight flinch. Had there been some trouble with the law in her past? Was that what made her nervous about this building?

"Occupations were not exactly upstanding, either. Two of them worked at exotic dance clubs somewhere in Phoenix or the surrounding areas. One worked at a diner that is known to be a hot area for solicitation." Jennison grinned slyly at Kendrick.

Kendrick chuckled. "Yeah, I offered to do some undercover work at the clubs, but somehow couldn't clear it with my boss, much less my wife."

Brandon ignored the jokes. He wasn't surprised about the women's occupations. Quite often an arrest record accompanied such jobs.

"What exactly have you done concerning the investigation?" Brandon could hear the tightness in Andrea's tone.

"We've done our due diligence." Kendrick sat up a little straighter in his chair. "We interviewed employers, canvassed the area for witnesses, ran DNA and searched for any prints."

Jennison interjected. "Look, we appreciate Omega sending you down here, and if you come up with any insight we'd love to hear it. We don't want a killer wandering around loose. But the fact is, none of these women seem to have anyone who cares about them, two have an arrest record and all have employment that is a bit questionable."

Kendrick shrugged. "So basically, we'll do all we can—like Jennison said, nobody wants to let a killer go free—but we're not getting any pressure from the higher-ups to put major resources into this investigation. Unfortunately, these women were pretty much nobodies."

Chapter Four

These women were pretty much nobodies.

No family who cared. Arrest records. Questionable employment.

If the killer had been around four years ago, Andrea might have been one of the victims. Every part of that account described her when she was nineteen, before changing her life at Omega.

She wanted to, but she could hardly blame the cops. Law-enforcement funding was limited. Unfortunately, without family demanding justice, these murders, if not easily solved, would just get pushed to the side.

The only reason Omega had been called at all was because it was obvious the three kills had been performed by the same person. Otherwise Andrea didn't know if the locals would've put any true effort into finding the killer.

They were on their way now to The Boar's Nest, one of three bars here in Buckeye, where the latest victim—Noelle Brumby—had been known to frequent. It was two o'clock in the afternoon, but evidently Noelle had hung out here in the afternoons since she worked nights.

Andrea's weariness pressed against her—reviewing

the case files had taken her most of the night—but she pushed it aside. She had made it through talking to Lance Kendrick, who had thankfully not remembered her from her brief run-in with the sheriff's office for underage drinking years ago. She could make it through this.

Walking inside, she thought The Boar's Nest looked just the way someone would expect a small-town bar to look in the middle of the afternoon: dingy, run-down, pathetic. Night hid a lot of sins of this place that sunlight brought out.

The Tuesday afternoon crowd wasn't the most upstanding. Anybody who had a white-collar job, and even most of the blue-collar ones, would not be in this place at this time. The people patronizing The Boar's Nest now worked nights or didn't work at all.

Andrea heard a low whistle as they walked in, but didn't know if it was for her looks or because they were obviously law enforcement. Nobody ran for the exit or stopped any activities suddenly, so at least it didn't appear that anything illegal was happening.

She felt Brandon step closer to her and could see him looking around, obviously checking for any danger. Cops were sometimes not welcome in places like this, although that would not stop her and Brandon from their questioning. Brandon had a weapon, but Andrea didn't. Hopefully he wouldn't need to use it.

Two pool tables lined the far end of the room, with three guys playing on one. A bartender unpacked boxes and put glasses away behind the bar, and a couple sat at a table sipping beers in the corner.

All of them were looking at Brandon and Andrea. Brandon touched her gently on the back—she knew it was an unconscious habit more than anything else but it still sent a slight shiver through her—and they headed toward the bar.

The bartender looked at them without halting his motions. "Lost or cops?"

Brandon chuckled. "Can't be thirsty?"

"Yeah, you can. And I'll gladly get you something, but I'm still pretty sure you're one of the other two, also."

"You're right—the latter. We're investigating the death of Noelle Brumby."

The bartender stopped putting away the glasses. "Yeah, that was a damn shame. She was a nice girl. Friendly. I'm Phil. I own this bar."

Andrea studied Phil while he talked. He seemed very sincere about liking Noelle.

"Can you tell us anything else about her?" Brandon asked.

"She worked at a...er, gentleman's club closer in to Phoenix."

Allure. They already knew that and would be interviewing people there soon, even though Kendrick and Jennison had also spoken with them.

"Why didn't she work at Jaguar's, do you know?" Andrea was hesitant to bring up her former place of employment in front of Brandon, but understanding why Noelle would drive farther to work at a club rather than work at the strip club here in town might have some bearing.

Both the bartender and Brandon looked a little surprised at her question.

"You from around here?" Phil asked. "You've never

been in this bar before. I'm pretty sure I'd remember you."

"I've driven through town a few times." Better to just keep her past out of it.

"Noelle didn't like the owner over at Jaguar's. Had heard some bad things about him. Harry Minkley's his name."

Yeah, Andrea already knew Harry's name. And she was glad Noelle had the good sense not to work for him. Although in the long run, it hadn't helped her.

"Noelle came in here a lot?" Brandon leaned one arm against the bar so he had a better view of the whole place.

"Mostly during the week in the afternoons. Weekends were pretty busy for her, as were a lot of evenings. She hung out with those guys over there. The tall, skinny one's named Corey. Big one next to him is Luke and the other is Jarrod." He pointed back to where the three guys were playing pool. "They knew her better than me."

Brandon and Andrea both turned toward the men. "Thanks for your help," she said over her shoulder.

"Thank you for trying to find the killer." Phil turned back to his unpacking. "I wondered if anyone would bother."

The three younger men—all in their early to mid-twenties—continued to play pool as she and Brandon made their way over. But she could tell they were quite aware of her and Brandon as law enforcement and of her as a woman.

"Hey, guys." Brandon's tone was friendly but firm. "We'd like to talk to you about Noelle Brumby."

Andrea tried to watch all three as closely as she could. Two, Luke and Corey, immediately tensed, but she wasn't sure if that was because of their relationship with Noelle or because they just didn't like cops. The other one, Jarrod, definitely expressed some guilt at Noelle's name, but mostly couldn't seem to get his attention off Andrea.

Andrea tried to classify in her mind the reactions of each man. She wished she could record them and study them multiple times later, but she didn't have that luxury in this situation.

"What makes you think we even knew her?" Luke asked, now holding the pool cue with white knuckles.

"Phil said she hung out with you three a lot."

"Yeah, well, maybe Phil should keep his mouth shut," defensive guy number two—Corey—muttered, not looking up from the shot he was making.

Brandon walked around the pool table so he was standing against the far wall. Andrea understood why he did it, to get a different angle and perspective for reading these guys, but she felt more exposed without him next to her.

"We're trying to find the killer of someone who was your friend. I'd think you'd want to help with that." Brandon was watching Luke and Corey as he made the statement—one meant to cause a reaction. Andrea turned her attention to Jarrod, only to find him overtly studying her, so she looked back at the other two men.

"Some sicko killed Noelle," Luke said. "We don't know anything about it."

Corey was looking more and more uncomfortable.

"What's your name?" she asked softly even though she already knew.

"You don't have to answer that, Corey." Luke wasn't too smart.

Jarrod laughed from where he stood against the wall. "You just told her his name, Luke. Dumb ass." Of course, he'd just done the same thing.

"Corey—" Andrea took a step toward the other man "—do you know something? Anything that could help us find Noelle's killer?"

"No." Corey shook his head, not really looking at her. "I don't know anything."

Andrea was about to press further with Corey when Jarrod interrupted.

"Oh my gawd, are you Andrea Gordon?" Jarrod all but gushed. "It is you, right? You were in one of my math classes in high school. I'm Jarrod McConnachie."

Damn it. Andrea knew she might be recognized at some point, but hadn't thought it would be by some guys in a bar in the middle of the afternoon.

Luke tilted his head to one side. "Oh yeah, I think I remember you. You were pretty quiet. But always hot." All three men snickered.

Oh God, had they come to see her dance when she worked at Jaguar's? She'd always worn wigs and enough makeup to give herself an entirely different appearance, but the thought they might recognize her and announce it made her absolutely sick.

"I thought you'd moved away your junior year," Jarrod said.

She hadn't moved away, really just to the other side

of town. But she'd dropped out of school. "Yeah, something like that."

"But I still kept seeing your mom and dad around. So then I didn't know what happened to you. A couple people thought you'd died and they just hadn't announced it."

It was good to know a few people noticed she was gone.

"It was my aunt and uncle I lived with, not my mom and dad. But yeah, they stayed here when I left." They'd never once tried to find her, thank God. That last time when she'd fallen through the table, they had probably been afraid they might go to jail. Looking for her wouldn't have been in their best interest.

Andrea should've gone to the police. She knew that now. Knew there were good officers out there—Omega worked with them all the time—who wanted to help. Who would've believed her or at least have thoroughly investigated. But at the time she'd been young and scared and thought all cops were the enemy.

The exact way these guys thought of them, too. She needed to get the questions back on track but had no idea how to do so.

"Well, you sure cleaned up nice," Jarrod said, moving slightly closer. "And you're a cop. I'd be happy to let you cuff me to anything you want."

The other guys chuckled.

"How about if I cuff you and throw you in a cell with a couple of long-term criminals?" Brandon interjected, coming to stand next to Andrea again. "Would that work for you?"

"Look, man—" Jarrod backed off "—I was just trying to say hello to an old friend."

Brandon's eyes narrowed. "Instead, why don't all of you tell us where you were on Friday night between midnight and 4:00 a.m.?"

The body had been found Saturday afternoon, but the coroner put the time of death as late Friday night or early Saturday morning.

"I was at home with my wife," Corey said. Brandon marked it down in a notebook.

"I was in Phoenix at a bar with a bunch of friends," Luke said, giving its name. "We started home after last call." He glanced down before looking up defiantly at Brandon and Andrea.

There was definitely more to that story. Luke's emotions weren't necessarily guilt in a specific sense, but a sort of overall vague sense of shame.

"I was at my house sleeping, after walking home from here. I live off Old Highway 80," Jarrod said, still staring openly at Andrea.

"You live alone?" Brandon asked.

Both the other men snickered. Brandon raised an eyebrow. "What?"

"No," Luke said. "He lives with his mother."

Jarrod turned away, grimacing. "Thanks, Luke."

Andrea couldn't help but smile a little at Jarrod's comeuppance. Especially since his desire to bed her practically oozed from his pores. He wasn't even trying to hide his craving for Andrea.

"Your mom can vouch that you were at the house?" Brandon asked Jarrod.

"Yeah, man. She's always at home. Gets so angry at me whenever I go out."

Probably pretty angry that Jarrod didn't have a job, either, but Andrea didn't mention that. Didn't want to draw the attention back to herself.

She watched all three men as Brandon got their names and contact information. He explained that, at this point, they were eliminating suspects. Telling the truth now would save them from more trouble later. Although none of them were thrilled at giving the info, none of them resisted.

Jarrod tried to talk to her while Brandon spoke with the other men, but she wouldn't engage with him. She'd had plenty of practice being standoffish over the past few years. Shutting him down was easy.

Plus, she wondered if he wasn't trying to get on her good side because he was hiding something.

One thing she knew for sure as she and Brandon left the bar, waving to bartender Phil as they went—all three men they'd interviewed today had secrets. All of them had lied or withheld information in some way.

Chapter Five

They spent the entire next day traveling around Phoenix and Buckeye, checking alibis, talking to the employers and colleagues of the women.

As the detectives had said, none of the victims had family who had spoken up. It didn't seem as if they had many friends, either. The killer had chosen well: women whose deaths would go relatively unnoticed. Only the ritualistic placement of the bodies and the symbolic items found with each victim even clued in law enforcement that it was the same killer at all.

The killer probably hadn't been able to stop himself from placing the symbols of purity around the women, even if he'd intellectually recognized that it could lead to his demise. The purity rituals had been just as important to the killer as the kill itself.

The killer was calm, sure of himself—almost definitely a *he* based on the nature of the crimes and the fact that the victims were all females. These murders hadn't been done in rage. There had been no mutilation of the bodies, no bruising beyond the restraints on the wrists and the rope marks around the throat.

If he let himself, Brandon could perfectly envi-

sion the rope tightening around the victims' throats.
The killer most certainly would've had them on their
knees—an act of repentance, needed before one could
be deemed pure.

The killer hadn't been interested in the women sexually—or perhaps he had and wouldn't let himself act
on it—only in freeing them from their evil. Cleansing them.

Brandon had been sitting in his hotel room for the
past hour, looking blankly ahead. To most people it
would've seemed as if he was staring out into nothing, but really he was giving his mind a quiet place to
sort through all the data he'd been processing for the
past forty-eight hours.

Letting his mind get into the head of a killer.

It wasn't a comfortable place to be, and since David's death, Brandon didn't let himself get in that dark
place too often.

Brandon was aware of the dark side of his intelligence, of his nature. Was well aware that immersing
himself deep into the thoughts of a killer could leave
him tainted by that darkness.

And now there was no one to drag him back but
himself. No one to warn him when he was getting too
close to the abyss. It was one of the things he missed
most about having a partner he trusted.

And speaking of partners, it was time to meet his
temporary one. When they'd arrived back at the hotel,
Andrea had all but fled into her room. She'd said it was
because she wanted to look over some notes from today's interviews, but Brandon knew that couldn't be
it. She hadn't taken any notes all day.

She was an enigma. Her work ethic seemed impeccable—she was punctual, attentive and focused—but then she'd do something completely unprofessional like refuse to take any notes.

Even Brandon took notes. He realized a long time ago his brain—all brains—were capable of great things, but they were never infallible. Evidently Andrea thought hers was the exception.

He should be thankful for her flaw. For her reminder that he didn't want someone like her as a partner. Because if he woke up one more time, his body hard and wound up, dreaming about her—about kissing her and removing all the professional clothes she wore like armor—he was afraid he would act on it.

He needed to keep his distance.

Pulling rank and forcing her to have dinner with him was not helping with that plan. She'd wanted to camp out in her own room all evening, grab some crackers, go over what they'd found. He'd told her they needed to eat real food and could discuss the case while doing so. She put up a bit of an argument, but he hadn't listened, just threatened to bring dinner to her hotel room so they could work there.

That got her agreement.

He moved into the lobby to meet her. They were going to walk a few blocks down the street to the mom-and-pop Italian restaurant. He saw her as she walked in the lobby just moments later. He had changed into jeans and a T-shirt, but she still wore her pants and blazer from the interviews earlier. She looked nice, no doubt about that. But definitely not casual or comfortable. He wondered if she ever looked casual or comfortable, if she ever just let herself relax around anyone.

He couldn't seem to make himself stop looking at her. Damn, he wanted to peel her out of those clothes. To see if there was any fire underneath and disprove the ice-queen theory. To show her that it was okay to *let go* with him. To protect her from whatever demons she was fighting. The sudden overwhelming thoughts caught him off guard.

"What?" she asked at his continued stare.

"Nothing. Just hungry. Ready?"

After walking to the restaurant and ordering, Andrea immediately brought up the case, obviously wanting to offset the chance of talking about anything personal. That was fine with Brandon. He hoped to use this time not only to go over the case, but to give her a lesson in law enforcement about the need to take notes. He wanted to point out how many things she missed by not taking notes and trying to keep it all in her head.

"So what do we know about each of the victims? Let's make sure we haven't missed any details," he said as the waitress brought their salads and they began eating.

Andrea nodded. "Victim one, Yvette Tyler, found two weeks ago. Twenty-one years old, brunette, five feet five inches, 115 pounds. No family. Place of employment—Diamond Cabaret Strip Club in Phoenix."

Her lips pursed the slightest bit with that sentence. Evidently she didn't approve of that career choice.

Brandon continued. "She was arrested last year for drunk and disorderly, and underage drinking, but since she had no record the charges were dropped."

"Yes. Victim two, Ashley Judson, found six days ago. Eighteen years old, worked at a diner west of here in Tonopah on I-10."

"That truck stop is known to be a place for truckers to pick up women, and women to pick up rides, literally and figuratively."

Andrea smiled a little at that and speared another bite of her salad. "Judson had also been arrested for solicitation, no surprise there. Spent a couple of nights at the Maricopa County lockup, too. Charges were dropped because of some technicality."

"And we have Noelle Brumby."

"Yes, twenty-three, blond. Worked at Allure in Phoenix."

She knew her facts better than he'd thought. Maybe he'd misjudged her at the airport when he'd thought she was just skimming over the files.

The waitress brought their main course. Andrea had ordered chicken Alfredo; Brandon had gotten lasagna. He had to admit, it smelled delicious.

"So give me your opinion of Noelle's friends, the guys at the bar yesterday. Jarrod and the other two."

"Luke and Corey," she murmured, taking a bite.

Hmm. That had been his first attempt to catch her, to use as an example later of why she should take notes. Guess that wouldn't work.

"They're all hiding something," she said.

"Something about Noelle's death?"

She shrugged. "Tied to it, probably yes, although I don't think any of them are the killer."

Interesting. "Okay, tell me what you saw and what you concluded."

"Corey looks most guilty at first glance. Or at least he feels guilty about something."

Brandon had noticed that, also. "Go on."

"I think he was either having an affair with her or was in love with her or both. His guilt probably stems from a lot of things—failure to help Noelle, his feelings about cheating on his wife, not being able to do anything about it now."

"I agree."

She nodded. "And he's scared. That's what initially made me think he might be the killer, but I think he's scared that his wife is going to find out. That the investigation will uncover the affair."

"What about the defensive guy, Luke?" He took a bite of his lasagna. It tasted as good as it smelled. "You think he's hiding something, too?"

"He definitely has no love for law enforcement."

Brandon chuckled; that had been clear enough for a blind person to see.

"He also didn't want us looking into his alibi at the bar."

That was interesting. Something he hadn't picked up on.

He slowed his chewing. "Okay, why do you think that? His alibi checked out today."

She shrugged. "He definitely had a vibe, something he didn't want discovered. After talking to the bartenders today, I think it was probably that he and his friends drove home drunk. They were definitely drinking enough to be drunk, and then according to his own testimony he drove himself home."

A good insight.

She took another bite. "Or his guilt may have been about some sexual shenanigans they got into. Maybe he seduced some girl in the bathroom and feels a little bad about that—I don't know." She couldn't quite keep eye contact with him as she said it.

She couldn't look at him when talking about sex. Maybe he wasn't the only person affected when the two of them were together. Maybe Little Miss Professional wasn't as buttoned-up as he thought.

"Okay, interesting theories."

"But not pertaining to the case, so not important." She frowned and stabbed her pasta with more force than necessary.

"I didn't say that. Understanding—getting inside their heads, their desires—can lead you to the right path. It's not always a direct route, but it almost always helps."

She shrugged. "Only if it's the actual criminal. Otherwise you're wasting time."

"Eliminating someone isn't a waste of time. It's one step closer to the truth."

"Well, I don't think either Luke or Corey are our killer. I think they're up to no good in at least some part of their lives, but not killing."

"And Jarrod?"

"I didn't really get a read off him, one way or another. He was embarrassed to still be living at home, I know that."

Brandon had gotten a read off Jarrod. Not because of his skill as a profiler, but because he was a man.

Jarrod wanted Andrea. It had pretty much consumed the man's thoughts. That neither cleared him nor made him guilty. His mother had told them that Jarrod was home when they talked to her today, but she had to admit, she hadn't actually been in the room with him during any of the hours in question.

Jarrod could've come home then sneaked back out.

Of course, nothing about Jarrod matched the profile Brandon was developing in his mind. Jarrod wasn't methodical or meticulous like the killer, so Brandon wasn't looking at the younger man as a true suspect yet. However, Brandon still might find reason to arrest him if he kept making moves toward Andrea.

"So did you know Jarrod well in high school?" Brandon wasn't sure why he'd asked, but he knew he wanted to know.

The fork that was carrying food to her mouth stopped and returned to the plate without the bite being eaten.

"No. To be honest, I don't remember him at all."

"He said he was in your math class."

She shrugged, fidgeting slightly in her seat. "A lot of high school was just a blur for me. You know how it is."

Brandon wanted to know more about her. "What clique were you? Sports? Nerd? Punk rocker?"

A ghost of a smile passed her lips. "None, really. I pretty much kept to myself."

Like the way she pretty much had kept to herself the past couple of years while at Omega?

She was pushing her food around on her plate now, not really eating it. Okay, she didn't want to talk about high school. Maybe she had bloomed more in college. That happened. For some people high school had been a miserable experience. Brandon's own high school experience had been nothing fantastic.

But now Brandon found he wanted to know something about Andrea. Something about her as a person. Not about her abilities as a behavioral analyst—hell, he was already completely impressed by just about everything she'd done concerning the case. His plan to teach her about note-taking had just proved fruitless; she'd taught him a lesson about her abilities instead.

But what did he really know about her? Name, occupation, age. Brandon made a living getting inside the minds of others, but he'd be damned if he'd been able to do so with her.

Brandon eased back into info and tactics he'd learned in his basic psychology classes way back in undergrad: get someone comfortable with you if you wanted them to freely share information. The best way to do that was a compliment.

That was easy with Andrea. Her skills were impressive.

"I think everything you've said about the guys tonight is spot-on. You caught a few things I missed." He wasn't faking any sincerity when he said it. "And I like to think I don't miss very much."

He could see the tension ease out of her torso even from across the table. She really didn't want to talk about high school. Maybe it was just being here in town; maybe it was something she never wanted to talk about. Brandon wouldn't push.

He smiled at her. "Steve was right about your abilities. It's impressive."

She smiled back at him, obviously basking in his

praise. That was something for him to file away. It confirmed what Steve had told him in his office on Monday. Andrea still wasn't sure about herself and exactly where and how she belonged in Omega.

Which was a shame. Someone with her abilities should rest very comfortably in them. It would make her a better analyst if she wasn't constantly second-guessing herself. Brandon found himself wanting to help her with that.

To make Omega a stronger law-enforcement entity, of course. It had nothing to do with getting closer to the woman sitting across from him, with seeing more of her smiles, seeing her relax and ease into her own abilities.

He forced himself to tear his eyes away from hers and eat the last bite of his food.

He would start on neutral territory.

"So, where'd you go to college? Did you decide to study criminal science or end up going with psychology?" It had been a question he'd had to choose, but had found he couldn't decide, so he'd ended up studying both.

"I, um...I—"

Brandon looked up from his plate and found all of Andrea's tension back. More. She was biting her lip and pulling at her blazer sleeve.

Evidently the subject of college was even worse than high school.

"Andrea—"

She stood up, her chair scraping loudly on the floor. She flinched. "Brandon, I'm sorry. I have to go. I'm not feeling well."

"Just wait and I'll—"

"No. I'm sorry, no—"

She was gone, hurrying out the restaurant door before he could stop her.

Chapter Six

Brandon paid the bill a few minutes later, trying to figure out what had just happened. He replayed the conversation in his mind to see if he'd said anything that could be construed by Andrea as offensive or threatening.

All he'd really done was ask her about high school and college.

Brandon had been studying people long enough to know her behavior signified more than just a desire not to talk about herself. It came back to what he had argued about with Steve in his office.

Andrea Gordon had secrets. And they had to do with this town.

What Brandon didn't know was if he should press or not. Her secrets, whatever they were, didn't seem to get in the way of her doing her job. He had no complaints about the insights she was bringing into the case.

But the man inside him—his basic, most primal man—could not abide that she was hiding things from him. That she had pain, that she needed help, and she would not share that with him. He wanted to force her to tell him so he could fight the battle for her.

Brandon grimaced as he sat back in his chair. He

knew himself well enough to know there were parts of his psyche that he didn't allow to break through very often, but were still quite strong inside him.

The part of him he called the warrior.

The warrior kept things very simple, saw only in black and white, right or wrong. Not the shades of gray that his intellect wandered in all the time. The warrior inside was who kept Brandon from becoming a criminal himself.

The darkness and the warrior combated each other.

God knew he came by the warrior honestly. He had literal fighter's blood flowing through his veins from his ancestors on both sides: Japanese samurai from his father's side, Scottish clansmen from his mother's.

The warrior wasn't interested in profiling or studying nonverbal cues. He wasn't interested in what was politically correct or even polite. He was interested in fighting for what was *just*. What was *his*.

Brandon didn't let the warrior side of himself come to light very often. He preferred to use his intellect and reasoning abilities to get things done.

But when it came to Andrea, the warrior kept pushing his way forward.

Well, that was too damn bad, because Brandon wasn't about to let his Neanderthal self run roughshod over this entire investigation. Brandon had to work with Andrea. She was his partner, for however long this case lasted. He would not go demanding answers from her.

Demanding kisses from her.

But he would go find her and make sure she was okay. Let her know he wasn't going to push her to talk about things she wasn't ready to share.

The warrior inside all but growled, but Brandon ignored him, pushing him back down.

Brandon exited the restaurant and walked back up the block toward the hotel. And, just his luck, it was starting to drizzle hard enough to be an annoyance.

He almost didn't see Andrea.

Of course, he wasn't looking for her to be standing on the edge of the parking lot since she'd left the restaurant ten minutes ago. But she was, staring at a car—an old beat-up Chevy—parked close to the hotel's front entrance.

She wasn't moving, just standing in the rain. Frozen in what seemed to be terror.

Brandon's first thought was that it was Damian Freihof, the would-be bank bomber. Had he found Andrea here? But then he realized Freihof wouldn't be sitting in a car and Andrea wouldn't just be staring at him if he was.

He walked up to Andrea, careful to come at her slowly and from the side so he didn't sneak up on her in any way.

"Hi." He kept his voice even, calm. "What are you doing out here? Everything okay?"

She looked at him then back at the parking lot.

Without being obvious about it, Brandon withdrew his weapon from the holster at his side. Had she seen something to do with the case?

"Andrea." His voice was a little stronger now. "What's going on? Is it something to do with the murders? Did you see something or did someone threaten you?"

She kept staring.

"Andrea, look at me."

She finally turned to him, hair plastered to her head from the rain, makeup beginning to smear on her face.

"I need you to tell me what's happening. Is there danger? Did you see something having to do with the case?"

Andrea's eyes finally focused on Brandon. "N-no. No, there's no danger. I just…I just thought…" He waited but she didn't finish her sentence.

Okay, not an immediate danger and nothing from the investigation. Something from her past, then. He holstered his weapon. There wasn't danger, but she needed help. Especially since she didn't seem capable of taking care of herself at the moment.

"Let's go inside, sweetheart." The endearment slipped out unbidden. "Let's get you out of the rain."

She stiffened. "No, I can't go inside." Her attention narrowed again on the old car parked near the front entrance, under the hotel's overhang. It looked as if someone was sitting inside, but it was too far for Brandon to get any details.

He and Andrea couldn't stay out in the rain—even the desert of Arizona was cold in March. Andrea was already shivering.

The car seemed to be the center of her terror, not the hotel.

"What if we go in the side door?" Brandon pointed to a door nearer to them. It wasn't close to their rooms, but it would at least mean not having to go in the main entrance through the parking lot.

She looked over at the door he referred to and nodded. Brandon wrapped an arm around her slim form and led her to the door. Once inside he kept her in his grasp as they made their way down the hall. She was still shivering.

Warrior or not, there was no way Brandon was letting Andrea out of his sight right now. He wasn't even sure he could let her out of his arms.

He stopped at his room and got his key card out of his pocket. He knew Andrea was in bad shape when she didn't protest him bringing her into his room.

He shrugged off his jacket and threw it over the chair, then helped her take off her soaked blazer and eased her down to sit on the edge of the bed.

He left her for a moment to go get a towel from the bathroom. When he came back she hadn't moved at all, was still sitting, huddled into herself, where he'd left her.

His heart broke a little bit at her flinch when he put the towel around her and began gently drying her hair.

"Shh. I won't hurt you. I just want to make sure you don't get sick." He took a corner of the towel and wiped it across her cheeks in an effort to dry them and also remove some of the makeup that had run down her cheeks. Her green eyes just stared out at him.

Brandon left the towel wrapped around her shoulders and grabbed a chair so he could set it right in front of her. He sat so they were eye to eye.

"Who was that in the car out front?"

He heard the tiny hitch in her breathing. "You saw it?"

"No, I could just see that *you* saw whoever it was."

"That's my aunt and uncle's car. They raised me after my mom died when I was ten."

"And you don't want them to know you're here?"

A shudder racked Andrea. "No. I don't ever want to see either of them again."

She looked away and began rubbing her arm, repeatedly. He looked down and saw scars, multiple small lines all around her elbow. He'd never seen the scars before but then realized it was because he'd never seen her without a long-sleeved shirt or blazer.

Her professional wardrobe was not just an emotional barrier between her and the world; it was a physical one.

As he looked down at the scars again, at her countenance, her posture, a rage flooded him. She had been abused.

He immediately tamped down his anger, knowing she would read it and could take it the wrong way. She needed support right now. Gentleness. Caring.

"They hurt you." His voice was barely more than a whisper, but it wasn't a question.

"They're alcoholics. And whenever they drank… My uncle mostly. My aunt just locked herself in her room."

A tear rolled down her cheek as she looked away from him out the window. She was still rubbing her arm.

"I know they can't hurt me now. I'm older. Stronger. Not the same person who lived in their house."

"All of that is true. Every word."

"And you could arrest them if they tried anything." She was obviously trying to give herself a pep talk.

He nodded. "I wouldn't hesitate to do so."

"I was so young and stupid. They didn't want me after my mom died, but I didn't have anywhere else to go. I tried to stay out of their way as much as possible. But in a way, I guess I should be thankful for them."

Brandon couldn't think of a single reason why an abuse survivor should be thankful for what she'd been through.

She shrugged. "It's because of my uncle that I learned to read people so well. The situation at home forced me to really study nuances of expressions."

"So you could stay a step ahead of his fists."

She nodded. "But it didn't always work. Sometimes you knew what was coming, but you couldn't escape it."

She was referring to her situation in second person instead of first—distancing herself. It was a coping strategy.

"The situation at home may have helped you hone your skills at a younger age than you would have otherwise," he agreed. "But I imagine your gift at reading people still would be there. You would've always been an extraordinary behavioral analyst—you just wouldn't have known about it until later in your studies."

Suddenly some of her earlier words and actions clicked into place for Brandon. Her defensiveness about college, the reason she had given him two different graduating years for high school.

"You ran away, didn't you?"

She flushed, embarrassed. "Yes. I was about to turn seventeen. My uncle came in, drunk, and pulled me from a sound sleep, throwing me off the bed before beginning to whale on me. I got out, after falling through a glass table. But I never spent another night in that house."

Rage coursed through Brandon. The temptation to go out there and give her uncle just the slightest taste of his own medicine almost overwhelmed him. But he ratcheted his temper under control.

Andrea needed him here.

"Good for you."

She rolled her eyes. "Sure, except for the fact that I had to drop out of high school. I was never any good at school anyway." She seemed to shrink into herself. "I'm dyslexic, so reading was—still is—hard for me."

Brandon grimaced. Dealing with dyslexia was a challenge for any child. And a child who had no academic or emotional support at home? A setup for failure. He thought about how he had mentally criticized her for not reading the police file at the airport. Now he knew why. Reading it would be difficult enough for her; reading in a crowded place with a bunch of distractions would be nearly impossible.

"Steve Drackett and Grace Parker, the head psychologist for Omega, met me in Phoenix when I was nineteen. I helped them with a bank hostage situation."

Brandon nodded, leaning closer to her and taking the hand that was still rubbing at her scars. He gently ran his fingers along her knuckles, not sure if he was trying to soothe her or himself. He knew about the bank, or at least about Damian Freihof. At this moment Brandon completely agreed with Steve's decision not to tell Andrea about Freihof. Buckeye was hard enough on her without adding the possible threat of a madman.

"They had me do some testing, because Steve was sure I had a natural ability at reading people."

"Behavioral and nonverbal communication diagnostic," Brandon murmured, not letting go of her hand.

"You know it?"

"I'm familiar with it." More than. He'd helped develop the latest, most thorough version of it when he'd been in grad school ten years ago. She'd taken the test he'd helped create.

"So you ran away to escape an impossible home situation and had to quit school. Steve and Grace realized how naturally gifted you were and brought you into the Omega fold."

She glanced down for just a second before looking at him again. "Yes, pretty much."

There was other stuff she wasn't telling him—glancing down rapidly was almost always a tell of hiding something. Amazing that she could read so clearly the emotions and microexpressions of others, but couldn't control them in herself.

But mostly what she felt, what every nonverbal element of her body language and facial expressions spoke for her, was shame.

"I'm not really your typical Omega caliber person, right?" She smiled crookedly, not quite looking him in the eyes. "No education, no training. Can't even read right. Afraid to face an old couple in a car."

Those sentences explained so much about her and her behavior over the past few years at Omega. She wasn't standoffish or an ice queen; she was an abuse survivor. She'd been keeping herself apart so her colleagues wouldn't find out about her past, afraid they would consider her unworthy of being part of the Omega team.

Brandon couldn't stop himself. He let go of her hands to cup her face, gently wiping her still-damp hair back from her cheeks.

"A few people might have thought that at first, but

no one would think it now, given your track record with cases."

She just shrugged.

He trailed his fingers down her cheek. The warrior in him happy to have her close, to finally know some of her pain so he could try to protect her. "You have a *gift*. Steve recognized it so thoroughly that he brought you—an unknown teenager—into Omega. And he has never regretted that decision, I'm positive."

"But I don't have any education. Any training."

"You can get both of those if you want it—you have plenty of time. Hell, if I could naturally do what you do? I would've stopped going to school when I was ten."

A ghost of a smile, but at least it was a *real* one. Brandon wasn't sure he'd ever seen anything so beautiful. He got up and sat next to her on the bed so he could put his arm around her. He had to be closer to her.

"I did get my GED a couple years ago," she murmured, leaning into him. "And have taken a few semesters of college courses. But the dyslexia makes it hard."

"Of course it does," he said against her hair, pride running through him. "But you've persevered. You'll take it slow and finish as you're able. With your abilities, getting a degree is no big rush."

Brandon slid them back so they rested against the headboard of the bed. He kept his arm around her for support, but also because he couldn't seem to force himself to put any distance between them. She didn't seem to want it, either.

He wondered how long it had been since someone had just held her like this.

If ever.

He could feel her relaxing into him. Tension easing out of her body.

"I suppose I should go see if my aunt and uncle are still out there. I shouldn't be surprised they heard I'm in town. Gossip runs pretty freely around here." She shrugged. "I don't want to see them. Don't know why they would want to see me. But I guess I've got to face them sometime."

He tilted her face from where it rested on his shoulder and kissed her. Gently. Tenderly. His passion was there, just below the surface, but he kept it under tight rein—his passion was not the emotion he wanted her to pick up on. She didn't need that.

"Yes, but not tonight. You face them on your time, when you're ready. Not a minute before."

She sighed sinking back into him, nodding. Brandon wrapped his arms more tightly around her, wanting to keep her safe from anything that would ever cause her harm.

Chapter Seven

Andrea woke up with a start, eyes flying open. It was dark. She always slept with a light on, mostly because she didn't want to wake up like this: panicked, braced for violence. She didn't move, but held her body tense, ready to shoot off in whichever direction would get her to safety.

Slowly realization dawned. There was no danger here. The opposite, in fact. She was lying on top of the bedcover, wrapped in Brandon Han's arms.

They'd shifted a little in their sleep; he pulled her more closely to him so that she was draped nearly all down his side. Her leg was even hooked over his thighs.

Like lovers.

The thought of Brandon as her lover sent little explosions of passion barreling up and down her spine. She could think of nothing she wanted more.

She'd told him about her home situation. About not finishing school. About not having the education or background to really be a part of the Omega team. None of it had seemed to matter to him.

Of course, she hadn't mentioned she'd also been a stripper for a period of eighteen months—the worst eighteen months of her life. Some of those girls had thrived on being onstage, being the center of attention, driving men wild. For Andrea it had been an exercise in agony every time.

It was a part of her life she'd just as soon forget. And she couldn't think of a reason why she would need to tell Brandon, or anybody at Omega, about it.

She wanted to stay here in his arms, to sleep with him, to wake up with him and kiss him in the way she'd dreamed of. And much more than that.

Now that her eyes had adjusted to the darkness, she could see his chiseled features illuminated by the cloudy moonlight floating through the window. Black hair, prominent cheekbones, soft lips relaxed in sleep.

Despite his earlier, gentle kiss and the fact that he held her in his arms even now, Andrea didn't think Brandon was interested in her sexually. He was a colleague, perhaps could even be a friend. His emotions last night had radiated concern and sympathy for her, and even anger directed at her past.

Not passion.

Andrea eased her way back from him slowly. She should leave now. There was no need to have an awkward morning-after when they hadn't really had the fun part of the night before.

She worked herself away from him and out of the bed without waking him. She grabbed the shoes she'd taken off and her blazer from the chair. With one last look at his sleeping form, she slipped out the door.

A FEW HOURS LATER, in the hotel's dining room, Brandon slid into the chair across from Andrea. It didn't take any special reading ability for her to see he was pretty irritated.

"You snuck out in the middle of the night," he said as he added a creamer packet to his paper coffee cup.

Andrea would've thought he'd be relieved, not mad.

"Yeah, I woke up and thought it would be better if I went to my own room."

He tilted his head to the side and studied her.

"What?" she asked.

"I'm surprised you were able to get out without me waking up."

She shrugged. "I'm good at moving very quietly." A skill she'd picked up when not waking her drunk uncle had been a priority.

He still didn't stop staring at her. It was making her uneasy.

"Did you sleep okay?" he finally said. "Yesterday evening was a pretty rough one for you."

Her discomfiture came rushing back. She never should have told him all that stuff about herself. Sure, last night he'd been supportive, but this morning... Maybe this morning he realized what a fraud she really was.

He reached over and grabbed her hand, squeezing it just short of being painful. "Hey, whatever is going on in that mind of yours right now, stop."

"But—"

Now his eyes were mad. "I mean it. The only one thinking bad things about you at this table is *you*. So stop."

"Okay." She took a breath. He was right. She needed to learn to stop her self-sabotaging thoughts.

"So I'll ask you again—did you sleep okay?"

Did he mean before she left his room or afterward? She had slept amazingly in his bed. In his arms. But she probably shouldn't announce that, since he might think she was trying to get an invitation to do it again. Once she'd gotten back to her room the bed had seemed too big, too empty. She'd slept, mostly from the sheer exhaustion of having stayed up nearly all night on Monday studying the case files, but not nearly as well.

"I slept fine. Thanks." Seemed like the safest answer.

She had gotten up a little early to make sure she had time to do her hair and makeup perfectly. She was wearing the suit she knew she looked most professional in. After what had happened yesterday, Andrea had felt the need to show she was as competent and proficient as possible. To Brandon and herself.

"So what's our agenda for the day?" she asked briskly.

Brandon's eyebrow rose at the question. Andrea knew she was probably being a little too sharp, but she had to find a way to get them back on neutral footing.

Thankfully Brandon took her cue.

He sat up straighter. "We need to talk to the rest of victim number two's coworkers at the diner. See if any of them remember Ashley talking to someone in particular, not only that night, but the nights leading up to her murder. Find out if she had any regulars. That might be more difficult since none of them want to admit they're turning tricks on the side."

"It's probably not a regular who killed her since—"

Her sentence was cut off when both of their phones started vibrating.

"Damn it," Brandon muttered, looking down at the

email message that had popped up on his phone. "Maricopa Sheriff's Department found another body. Another girl has been murdered."

They were in the car and headed toward the crime scene five minutes later. Brandon called and updated Omega as they drove, promising to give more details as they became available. They didn't have far to drive. The body had been found just on the outskirts of Buckeye, again in front of another church.

Andrea glanced at Brandon. "Just so you know, I don't do crime scenes very often. My talents are with witnesses."

He nodded. "Yeah, I guess dead bodies don't give off many nonverbal cues for you to read."

"Honestly, I haven't really been around any." This was just another example of how untrained she was.

"Hey, a lot of agents try to get out of crime scenes—especially those with a dead body—any way they can. You know Liam Goetz, right?"

Andrea had worked with him and his pregnant soon-to-be wife, Vanessa, on a human-trafficking case a few months ago. He was head of Omega's hostage-rescue team—and had proved his skills rescuing a group of young girls who had been kidnapped and were about to be sold into sexual slavery.

"Yeah, I know Liam." She didn't know him well, but liked the big, muscular man and how caring he was with petite Vanessa, who was now huge with the twins she was carrying.

"He'll be the first to tell you that he doesn't mind putting bad guys in body bags—that man loves his guns—

but he will keel over every time he's in a coroner's exam room or there's a body at a crime scene he has to attend."

Andrea laughed just a little at the thought of it.

"Yeah, go head, laugh," Brandon continued, smiling. "You're not the one who has to drag two hundred pounds of pure muscle over to the side to get him out of the way. We've started requesting he not attend any situation where there's a body being examined."

"So I guess you're telling me it's okay if I don't go into the crime scene with you."

"That's up to you. All I'm saying is that there are Omega agents who choose not to. We don't think any less of them for it."

Andrea did appreciate Brandon trying to put her at ease.

The parking lot of the church where the body had been discarded was completely blocked off by police—both Maricopa County and City of Phoenix officers. There was a buzz of excitement in the air.

With a fourth victim, no one could deny this was a serial killer, not that Andrea had any doubts before.

Brandon immediately walked over, showing his Omega credentials, and began speaking with the coroner. Lance Kendrick and Gerardo Jennison were here also, talking to each other and Brandon.

Andrea hung back. She didn't want to do something stupid like pass out from being too close to the body. Although the thought that Liam Goetz did so made her smile.

Andrea could still see where the dead woman lay from where she stood. Like the others, she was covered with a sheer white fabric and a lily had been placed in her hands. Andrea couldn't tell, but she would guess the woman had been strangled like the others.

Officers were moving all around her, canvassing the area for any clues that might have been left on the ground. Another two were attempting to get fingerprints from nearby surfaces.

When he saw her, Kendrick excused himself from Brandon and Jennison and walked over to her, purpose in his eyes. He'd remembered her; she had no doubt about it. She wanted to run, but knew it was no use.

"You're Andrea Gordon, Margaret and Marlon's kid."

His expression wasn't hostile or even condescending. If anything, it was sympathetic.

"Actually, they're my aunt and uncle, but yeah, my guardians."

"You looked so familiar, but it was so vague I thought it was a case, like you'd suggested."

Andrea shrugged.

"You look a lot different than your mug shot," Kendrick continued.

Andrea clenched her teeth. Was this it? The end of her career? Would Kendrick tell Brandon? Could someone with a criminal record even work for Omega?

"Once I saw that picture I knew where else I'd seen you. Coming in with your mom—well, I guess your aunt—to pick your uncle up after he'd been thrown in holding when he was too drunk to find his way home. Must have happened a dozen times."

Andrea shrugged again, turning away slightly.

"Uncle was a mean drunk, if memory serves. Maybe

those nights we threw him in holding we were doing you a favor, I'm thinking now."

They'd been a much better night's sleep, that was for sure, but Andrea didn't say anything.

"There were a lot of screwups where you were concerned, Ms. Gordon. I'd like to offer Maricopa County's apologies, my personal apologies, for that."

Andrea turned back to Kendrick, surprised.

He looked at her solemnly. "Sometimes you can't see the full picture, except in hindsight. The system failed you. But you seem to have done all right for yourself." He gestured at her outfit.

"You mean despite having a record?"

Kendrick smiled at that although there was still a lingering sadness in his eyes. "You don't have a record, Andrea. You got brought in for underage drinking, but were never formally charged. I think the arresting officer just did it to scare you into going straight."

"It worked. I still can hardly drink anything without feeling some panic."

The officer smiled. "Well, there's no official record of your arrest, outside our storage room. So you don't have to worry about that. I'm just sorry no one ever looked further into your situation earlier, before you ran away."

His regret was so authentic it was almost painful.

"Like you said, I did okay for myself. I have a good job where I make a difference."

"And you're very well respected, if Agent Han is anything to go by."

Andrea looked over at Brandon to find him gazing

at her, concern in his eyes. She smiled at him to offer reassurance.

Lance Kendrick made his apologies once again and expressed his happiness to be working with her. Then he left to go deal with things pertaining to the dead woman. Not long after, Brandon made his way over to her, the notebook where he wrote everything down open to details about the case.

"Everything okay? I saw Kendrick over here."

"Yeah, he remembered me. He's a good cop. A little rough around the edges, but he cares."

Brandon nodded. "I got the info about the victim. Twenty-two years old, from here in Buckeye." He flipped a page in his notebook. "Her name is Jillian Spires and she's another stripper. Worked at a club called Jaguar's."

Chapter Eight

Andrea had wisely hung back as Brandon had examined the body with the coroner. As he'd told her, there was no need for her to get close unless she wanted to. If she wanted to get more thorough in investigating, he could ease her into that later when they were back at Omega in controlled circumstances. It didn't need to be while she was standing around a group of people she didn't know.

Or maybe one she did. Brandon saw Lance Kendrick come up to Andrea and had kept an eye on them as they conversed. Now that Brandon knew more about Andrea's past, what she'd survived, he found himself much more protective of her. The warrior was protective of her, as was the intellectual man.

Not even to mention how angry *both* were when he awoke to find her gone. It had been all he could do not to storm down to where she was and demand her return to his room.

To his bed.

But he'd gotten control of himself. An icy shower had helped. By the time he'd made it to breakfast he'd been able to be civil. He'd gotten the warrior tamped down, buried.

But he hadn't been able to stop himself from keeping a close eye on her all morning.

Andrea's conversation with Kendrick had been civil. Whatever the older man had to say, she hadn't been upset by it.

Or so he had thought. Because when he came over to give Andrea the details about the dead girl, all the color had drained from her face. The police had told him the dead woman had a local address, and she was close to Andrea's age. Maybe Andrea had known the woman personally.

"Hey, are you okay?" He stepped closer and cupped her elbow, moving her so she was blocked from the eyes of the other cops. "You look shaky. Did you know Jillian Spires?"

Andrea closed her eyes briefly. "No. I didn't know her. She must have moved here after I left."

Brandon's eyes narrowed. Her statement was odd. Wouldn't you automatically assume you just hadn't run in the same circles? Buckeye was a small town, but not *that* small. There would certainly be people you didn't know. Why would Andrea assume Jillian had arrived after she'd left?

"Are you sure you're okay?" he asked again.

She shrugged. "Yeah. I'm fine. I'm just— These women are my age. Some of them younger. They may not have a lot of family, but they don't deserve to die like this."

Brandon agreed although he was sure that wasn't the entire situation going on inside Andrea's head.

"Maybe this one will have family. Kendrick will do a more thorough check as soon as they get back to the office."

"So what's our next step?"

"We have a home address and a work address for the club, Jaguar's, where she worked. I figure we should probably start with the home. See if we get any known associates from there."

Her nod was just a little too exuberant. "Yeah, her home is probably our best bet."

Brandon's eyes narrowed slightly once again. There was something off in Andrea's behavior. She was hiding something. He almost started questioning her about it, but then stopped himself.

It could be about what had happened between them last night. Or about being back in this town that held so many painful memories. Or about being at her first homicide crime scene.

There were a lot of reasons Andrea could be a little off. He'd cut her some slack.

"The locals will also be there processing the scene at her home, so it'll be crowded. But we'll see what we can find. Besides, I would imagine her place of employment isn't open at ten thirty on a Thursday morning."

She didn't say anything, just turned toward the car with him. The ride across town to Jillian's apartment was mostly in silence, also. Generally Brandon didn't mind silence. He preferred it to someone filling the car with inane chatter. But he couldn't help but feel as though Andrea was not talking in order to deliberately withhold information.

Privacy was her way, ingrained over the past few years of having to keep totally to herself. Just because he knew about her abusive past didn't mean she was automatically going to start sharing every thought that came through her mind. Which was fine.

Except there was something else going on, he knew it.

They worked through lunch, examining Jillian's apartment. She hadn't been a neat freak, for sure, which made going through her personal belongings more time-consuming. They did find two glasses on the cardboard box that doubled as a coffee table, one rimmed with lipstick, one without. That meant someone besides Jillian had been in here relatively recently. The locals would run prints.

If anything, Andrea got more quiet as they looked through the girl's apartment. Brandon knew this wasn't her area of expertise—objects rather than people—so he didn't really try to draw her into the investigation. She looked around, staying out of the crime-scene team's way. Brandon did similarly.

There were two boxes full of stuff—notes passed in high school, a yearbook, pressed flowers from dances, a few stuffed animals and other knickknacks. Obviously items Jillian cared too much about to give away, although none of it held any value. Andrea picked up the yearbook and began looking through it.

"She graduated four years ago. She's from Oklahoma City." She held out the page that showed Jillian's senior high school picture.

Young, smiling, very much alive.

"That gives us something to go on." Brandon took

a picture of the picture with his phone. "She looks different now, but we can still use this picture when questioning people."

"Maybe she has a family." Andrea's face was pinched.

"Maybe. Kendrick will definitely start inquiring there."

After they finished with the apartment, they hit a fast-food place for a very late lunch. As they were finishing, Kendrick called to say the Phoenix coroner was almost ready to go over the body with them if Brandon wanted to attend in case he had any questions. Brandon agreed.

At his words, the heaviness that had befallen Andrea since the discovery of the body seemed to lift a little.

"Um, I don't think I'm up to seeing a dead body twice in one day," she said. "What if we split up? You can head into Phoenix. I'll walk up to Jaguar's—it's only a few blocks from here—and start interviewing the girls as they come in for work."

Brandon nodded. "Yeah, that's a good idea." He trusted Andrea's ability. At the very least she could narrow down who they should talk to more. "They're probably more willing to talk openly with you."

She paled. "Why do you say that?"

Brandon tilted his head to look at her. Why was she reacting so strongly to his statement? "Because you're a woman. You're young. I would think you pose much less of a threat to them."

Andrea smiled, but it didn't reach anywhere near her eyes. "Yeah, absolutely. Good thinking."

Brandon stood. "Okay, I'll text you when I finish at the coroner's office and we can touch base."

They both walked out the door. "I'll just give you a ride, okay? No need for you to walk. The extra two minutes won't make any difference to Kendrick." There was no rush. A dead body wasn't going anywhere.

She tensed for just a second before shrugging. "Sure. Thanks."

Brandon drove the few blocks to the gentlemen's club, *gentlemen* being quite a loose term in this situation. At night he was sure it didn't look quite so run-down and cheap. But right now it just looked like a warehouse that nobody cared about. He felt bad that Jillian had worked here. Felt bad for any women who worked here.

Andrea was staring at the building with as much contempt as he was. Her lips were pale with tightness and her hands pressed against her stomach. For a moment he thought she wasn't going to get out of the car.

"I'm sure the front door isn't open yet. I'll go around to the side. Text me when you're done, and we'll make a plan like you said." Her voice was tight. She didn't look at him.

She was out of the car before he could check that she was all right. She stopped a few feet away, then turned and waved, giving him a slight smile.

Obviously code for: *I'm okay. I can handle this.*

Brandon pulled around and out of the parking lot. Four days ago he wouldn't have left her here alone. Wouldn't have trusted that she could do the job. Wouldn't have believed she wouldn't miss something. It was that knowledge that kept him driving toward Phoenix. He needed to show he trusted her professional abilities.

But everything in his mind insisted this situation

was wrong. That he was missing something obvious. Andrea hadn't been okay all day since they'd arrived at the crime scene.

No, actually, she seemed to have done okay with that, too. It was not until he had told Andrea the dead girl's name that she'd totally withdrawn into herself. Had she known the woman? Her statement about Jillian moving into town after Andrea had left still struck Brandon as odd.

But Andrea had been right, according to the girl's yearbook. Jillian had obviously been in Oklahoma City four years ago, and that was when Steve had brought Andrea to Omega.

So she didn't know the girl.

Then what was the cause of Andrea's reaction? Her *continued* reaction all day, because she certainly hadn't bounced out of it. It had only gotten worse.

Brandon tried to think of exactly what he'd said when he told Andrea the victim's name. As he figured it out, he cursed. Violently.

Andrea hadn't been reacting to Jillian's name. She'd been reacting to the other information he'd given her: Jillian's place of employment.

Jaguar's.

He spun the car around at the first available safe place on the road. He put his phone on speaker and dialed Kendrick.

"This is Lance Kendrick."

"Lance, this is Brandon Han. I have some stuff I'm looking into and will need to miss the meeting with the coroner."

"No problem. I don't think there's anything much

different than the other women. I'll email you his full report."

"Thanks."

"You need help with your lead?"

"No. I'll let you know if we find anything. Andrea and I are headed to Jaguar's now to interview Jillian's coworkers."

"We'll keep each other posted, then."

"Absolutely." Brandon ended the call. Right now he just wanted to get back to Andrea. To figure out what was going on there. Fifteen minutes after he'd left her—pale and tense—in the parking lot at Jaguar's, he pulled back in.

She'd known there was a side door and where it was.

Brandon cleared his mind from every thought. He didn't want to come to the natural conclusion Andrea's actions pointed toward. He walked toward the side door she'd mentioned and entered the building once he found the door propped open. He stood back in the shadows, close enough to hear but not easily be seen.

There was Andrea, surrounded by four different women, all of them crying and hugging her. They all talked over each other, about Jillian's death, the state of the club, how much they'd missed Andrea and how mad they were that she'd just left without telling anyone.

Brandon couldn't force the thoughts away any longer, his brain turned back on full force.

Andrea had been a stripper at Jaguar's.

Chapter Nine

Walking back into Jaguar's had been the most difficult thing Andrea had ever done. She was thankful Brandon hadn't been here to witness it because there was no way she'd be able to explain the terror that swamped her as she made her way to the side door from the parking lot.

How many times had she come through the door in the late afternoon just like this? Her apartment had been only a few blocks away, so she had walked most of the time, a bag full of skimpy outfits, wigs and makeup thrown over her shoulder.

The eighteen months she had worked at Jaguar's had been some of the worst of her entire life. She had hated every second of it. But after being attacked while living out of her car when she couldn't afford anything else from what she made working at a gas station, Andrea had decided her safety was worth more than her pride.

Working here had at least gotten her off the streets.

She hadn't expected anyone to remember her when she came back, or perhaps they would just be able to vaguely place her. After all, she'd pretty much kept to herself here, too. The instant recognition and warm greetings—hugs, in fact, from three girls—had definitely not been expected. A fourth girl, who didn't even know Andrea, didn't want to be left out and jumped into the fray.

At first they'd just held on to her and cried. They'd heard about Jillian's death and were sad, scared. Then they'd had questions. They all, just as Andrea remembered—one of the few fond memories she had of this place—talked over each other.

"You just left without saying goodbye."

"Oh my gosh, you look so fancy. Like a lawyer or something. Gorgeous."

"Do the cops know who killed Jillian?"

"You're not coming back to work here, right?"

Andrea tried to answer the questions as best she could when they were being fired so rapidly she couldn't figure out who was asking what.

"I work as a consultant for a law-enforcement agency called Omega Sector. We're looking into Jillian's death with the local police."

"You were always too smart to work here." That was Lily. Andrea remembered her. She was kind, sort of scatterbrained.

Andrea shrugged. "I don't know about that. I didn't even graduate from high school. Dropped out."

"You may not have been book smart, but you definitely had an awareness of people. Could tell what they were thinking and feeling. Downright spooky sometimes. I'm not surprised the cops scooped you up to work for them."

That was Keira. She wasn't in the hugging/crying circle, didn't have time for that sort of nonsense. She was two years older than Andrea and had been the closest thing Andrea had had to a true friend while working here.

Keira may have been the closest thing Andrea had had to a friend, ever.

Andrea removed herself from the circle of women and walked over to Keira.

"Hey," Andrea said softly. "I'm sorry I didn't say goodbye all those years—"

She was shocked as Keira pulled her in for a tight hug. "Don't apologize for taking your chance to jump this ship," she whispered in Andrea's ear. "If you had come back after having a chance to get out, I would've kicked your ass."

Keira grabbed Andrea by the forearms and pushed her back. "Let me look at you. You cleaned up exactly like I imagined you would." She put her forehead against Andrea's. "I'm so proud of you. So happy for you."

"Thanks, Kee. I have a great job."

"And a man who cares a great deal about you."

Andrea laughed. "Um, no. Unfortunately, the job didn't come with that accessory."

"You sure about that? Because there's one tall drink of water over there who can't keep his eyes off you. And his suit says law enforcement, too." Keira gestured toward the side door with her chin.

Andrea felt her stomach lurch and swallowed rapidly. Brandon was here?

"He's just a man, honey. Don't forget that. Ultimately, we hold the power," Keira whispered in her ear before turning to the other girls. "Ladies, I'd like to see you at the bar so we can go over tonight's set. You can talk to Andrea later."

The women murmured disappointment, but followed Keira over to the bar. Andrea finally forced herself to turn around. When her worst fears were confirmed, she closed her eyes.

Brandon stood, the shadows from the doorway casting a bleak hue over his already-dark features. There could be no doubt in his mind that Andrea used to be employed here. There was no other possible interpretation of what had just happened with the girls.

"Andrea."

She opened her eyes, surprised to hear him directly in front of her now. Almost within touching distance.

But not quite.

"You should've told me."

What could she say to that? She just shrugged.

"I thought you were going to Phoenix."

"Kendrick is going to email me the info instead. I had a feeling there would be more action back here."

Andrea gave a short bark of laughter that held no amusement whatsoever. "You definitely got that right."

"How is it even possible you worked here four years ago? I'm not licensed to practice law in Arizona, but I imagine the legal age has to be twenty-one."

Not licensed to practice in Arizona? That meant he had to be licensed to practice in some other state. Plus two PhDs? Andrea rubbed her eyes tiredly with her hand.

"I had a fake ID. You could dance at eighteen, but couldn't serve drinks. I soon discovered I could make a lot more money if I waited tables between my dances. The owner wasn't one to look too closely at the IDs we showed him."

Brandon's lips pursed. Disapproval all but radiated off him. Andrea wrapped her arms around her waist. She couldn't blame him for disapproving. She should've just told him everything up front last night. At least now he understood why she really could never be part of the Omega team.

She'd always known eventually someone would find out about this. She looked around the club, the deep bucket seats around the tables where girls gave individual dances, the stage shaped like a T with three poles. With all the lights on there was nothing sexy about it. Just coldness, hardness, crassness.

Yeah, she'd always known eventually someone would find out about this—the truth Steve Drackett and Grace Parker had always refused to see—and would know Andrea wasn't meant to be part of Omega Sector.

It looked as though Brandon Han had just become that person.

ANDREA LOOKED AS if she might shatter into a million pieces at the slightest touch.

He wanted to wrap his arms around her, to hold her, to assure her that everything would be okay. But the tension in her body language suggested she would reject the physical contact. So he took one step closer, but went no farther. Even then she looked as if she might bolt.

He shouldn't be surprised that Andrea had worked in a place like this, given her history. But try as he might, he couldn't imagine her on the stage. He'd been to his share of bachelor parties, and hell, *college*, so he'd been to strip clubs before. Andrea definitely had the looks and physique to be a dancer.

But nothing he knew about her personality or temperament suggested to him that she would've wanted to work at this place. Not like, say, the friend she'd been talking to, who seemed very comfortable in her own skin and able to easily manipulate the stage and men's desires. Not that it mattered either way.

The psychiatrist in him wanted to fire off a bunch of questions, to understand her psyche, to understand all the circumstances surrounding her working here. Although a lot of it he could probably piece together himself.

"You needed money after you ran away."

She nodded. "I was living in my car, working at a gas station. When I was almost attacked one night while sleeping, I knew I had to do something else. I happened to meet Keira and she told me about this place."

"It's understandable, Andrea. No one would blame you for that choice."

"Yeah, right." She slid by him to walk out the door but stopped when a man entered. Andrea backed up.

"What are you doing in here?" the man—big, greasy, gruff—asked. He turned toward the bar and yelled, "Keira, what are customers doing in here before we're open, damn it?"

He turned back to Andrea. "We're not open, so you'll have to come back lat—" His eyes bulged and a nasty grin spread over his face. "Wait a minute—I recognize you. If it isn't little Drea all dressed up."

"Hi, Harry." Andrea's voice was small. Her shoulders hunched, and Brandon could see her arms crossed over her stomach in a protective huddle.

This man frightened Andrea.

"You come back to work for old Harry, sweet girl? I hear we have an opening."

Brandon gritted his teeth in distaste. He wished he could arrest Harry for something right now. He hoped he could keep himself from pummeling him into the ground, this man who so obviously threatened Andrea.

The warrior stretched inside him.

"No, I—I…" She was having difficulty getting the words out. Getting any words out.

Brandon stepped up so he was flanking Andrea. His chest was right at her shoulder and he placed his hand on her hip, making sure she could feel him. She wasn't alone in this.

"I'm agent Brandon Han with Omega Sector. We're investigating the death of Jillian Spires. You, of course, are one of our prime suspects." That wasn't true, but Brandon felt no qualms whatsoever about the lie. "We'll need you to provide a detailed written analysis of where you've been for the past seven days."

Harry's mouth fell open, but he stopped leering at Andrea. That had been Brandon's ultimate objective.

"I, um." Harry blinked rapidly and turned his attention to Brandon. "For a whole week?"

Brandon nodded, using his hand on Andrea's hip to guide her behind him. "That's right. Every place you've been. Written down. We'll be back to get it tomorrow and maybe to bring you in for questioning."

Brandon had no doubt that if Harry contacted a lawyer, his counsel would tell him that he didn't need to do any of this. That unless law enforcement was going to formally charge Harry with a crime, he didn't have to do jack squat to cooperate.

But Brandon had a feeling that Harry, with his thinning hair made even more evident by the way he slicked it back, was too cheap to call a lawyer. So let him spend the rest of his evening stewing and writing.

Brandon looked over his shoulder to Andrea, relieved to see at least a little color coming back to her face. "Would you mind telling the ladies that we'll be back tomorrow to interview them? Ask if they could come in early afternoon so we can talk."

Andrea nodded and walked toward the bar.

Harry evidently decided to try the buddy-buddy approach with Brandon. "Even all buttoned up, you can imagine what that one looked like on the stage, can't you?" His grin was slimy. There was no other word for it.

"She's my colleague." Brandon clenched his fists.

"Well, let me tell you, there was something about her up there." Harry had no idea how thin the ice he skated on was. "She wore wigs and makeup, but you couldn't hide those big green eyes. Like a deer caught in headlights every time she was up there. Everybody loved it. Not that they were looking at her face once her ti—"

The warrior inside Brandon broke free. He was in Harry's face in less than a second.

"That woman over there is an important member of a prestigious law-enforcement agency. What she did when you hired her—illegally, I might add, since she was a teenager—holds no bearing whatsoever to her ability to do her job now."

Harry swallowed hard. Brandon barely refrained from grabbing the other man by his dirty T-shirt.

"If I hear one disrespectful word come out of your mouth again about her, I will personally see to it that every person you've ever hired, every license you have to operate and every code involved in running a business like this is investigated. And if there are any problems or discrepancies, you will be *shut down*."

Harry nodded.

"Okay, I told them." Andrea returned and touched Brandon on the arm. He took a step back from Harry. "They'll be ready tomorrow."

Brandon turned to smile at her. He knew she would be able to pick up what was going on between him and Harry and wanted to assure her it was okay. "Harry and I got some things straightened out, too. Isn't that right, Harry?"

"Um, yes, sir. We're all clear. I'll have what you need by tomorrow. Anything to help catch Jillian's killer."

Brandon took Andrea's arm and led her out the door.

Chapter Ten

Andrea was huddled against the car door, as far away from him as she could get in the small rental, as they drove back to town and the hotel. Brandon, despite his training, wasn't sure what to say to her. But he knew it had to be something.

Finally she solved the problem by speaking first.

"I should've told you I had worked at Jaguar's." Her voice was small. Tiny. Ashamed. Part of his heart broke.

Brandon shrugged. "Maybe you should've this morning after we found out Jillian worked there. But before then it was pretty much irrelevant."

She rolled her eyes. "Right. Because no one at Omega would care that I was an ex-stripper."

He pulled the car into the parking lot of the hotel and shut off the engine, turning to her. "If I had been a carpenter or a janitor when I was twenty years old, would it make you think any less of me as an agent now?"

"That's different."

"How is it different? Most of us had a life—some of us had completely different careers before we worked for Omega."

"It's not the same." She clenched her fists.

"Why?"

"I took off my clothes for money."

Brandon took a breath. Damn, he was pissed. And he knew she would be able to feel it. But his anger wasn't directed at her. He wanted to make sure she understood that.

"What you did was survive a situation most people never have to live through."

"Nobody at Omega is going to care about that."

Maybe it was time for a little tough love. "No offense, but nobody is going to care either way."

That got her attention. She spun her head toward him. "What?"

"You do your job well. That's all anybody at Omega cares about. You are an intelligent, gifted behavioral analyst."

"What I am is a runaway high school dropout, ex-stripper."

She got out of the car, so he did the same. Thankfully the parking lot was mostly empty. She stared at him across the hood of the car. At least there was some color in her cheeks and fire in her eyes. She didn't need sympathy and gentleness. That just encouraged the vulnerable side of her. She needed someone to tell it to her straight.

A friend.

Brandon wasn't sure she'd ever had one. Definitely hadn't had one at Omega. Well, he could be one for her.

He may be a turned-on friend, but he could be a friend.

"You forgot dyslexic."

Her eyes bugged out of her head. *"What?"*

"You're a runaway, dropout, *dyslexic* ex-stripper. Throw in an unfortunate shark attack and you've got yourself a pretty tragic tale there."

Now her eyes narrowed to slits. "Do you think I'm trying to get you to feel sorry for me?"

"No." Although God knew there was plenty to feel sorry for. "But I'm trying to get you to see the truth."

"That my past doesn't matter." Her lips tightened into a line. "You'll have to forgive me if I disagree."

She turned and began walking toward the side entrance of the hotel they'd used last night. Neither of them wanted to have this conversation coming through the main lobby. He jogged a few steps to catch up with her. Amazing how fast the woman could walk, even in heels.

"Of course your past matters. Everybody's past matters."

"That's easy for you to say. Your past is filled with schooling and degrees and graduations. Mine is filled with thongs and sleeping in my car and getting beaten by my uncle."

Brandon stopped her at the door. "Like it or not, our pasts are what make us who we are. But when it comes to Omega, you only want to concentrate on the bad parts of your past."

"That's because they're the most important parts."

"Says you. And you're stuck in your own head."

She started to reach for the door, but Brandon grabbed both her arms. He was gentle, but there was no way she was getting out of his grasp until he was ready to let her.

"You know what else is in your past? Four years of

helping Omega solve cases. Saving many lives and assisting in putting a number of criminals behind bars."

She shrugged, looking down. He put a finger under her chin and forced her face back up, ignoring the heat coursing through him.

"Not to mention you dropped out of high school but then got your GED, so I think you can stop using the dropout title. Plus you're actively going to college. At twenty-three, it's not like you're some grandmother going back to school."

He could tell he was getting through to her. Her posture was relaxing, her body angling more toward him.

He wanted her; he could feel it in the tightness throbbing through his body. He wanted to sweep her up in his arms and carry her down to his room like a grand romantic movie. Wanted to make love to her for days until neither of them had strength to move.

But more than that he wanted her to see the truth about herself. How much she brought to the table.

He released her chin when she nodded. She opened the door and they both walked into the hallway.

"It's hard for me to get past. Hard for me to think anyone else could get past it, either, especially at Omega. Best of the best and all that."

"I would argue that your talent, your ability to read people, makes you one of the best. And your past—even the part when you worked at Jaguar's—helped make you into who you are now and what you can do."

"I just wouldn't know how to tell anyone about it."

"Why would you have to? Have you ever been in a briefing where we all sat around talking about our complete history? No. Because that's not what matters. Tell people you waited tables. That was true, also."

"Yeah, I guess so."

He wanted to shake her. Or hug her. Or definitely kiss her, but knew it wasn't the time for that. "You have a natural gift. Everybody knows it, and no one questions it. You don't have to have an origin story to tell everyone."

She laughed a little. "That's good, because I'm not a superhero."

They were at her door. He wanted to say the most important thing before she left. "You don't have to tell anybody anything about your past. Most people won't ever ask, and hardly anyone would care even if they knew all the details."

She nodded slightly.

"But the true issue here, I think, is not even about what judgments people might make if they knew about your shark-attack past and the rest." He tried to keep it light, before making his ultimate point. "The true issue is that if you embrace your past and own it, you'll be forced to stop treating every good behavioral analysis choice you make like it's a happy accident."

Her head jerked up to look at him.

"Embracing, or at least accepting, your past means accepting your present and your future at Omega. It means having to trust people. Not about knowing your past, but about allowing you to make mistakes in your future and not hold it against you."

He kissed her forehead gently, although he wanted to do much more than that. "You hold yourself away from everybody to try to make yourself perfect. Being real, being part of a team, means showing others you're not. And giving them a chance to accept you in spite of that."

He stepped back from her. "The past doesn't have to control your future anymore."

Brandon turned to walk to his room. He heard Andrea's door click and hoped he hadn't said more than he should.

WAS BRANDON RIGHT? Had she kept her distance from everyone these years at Omega not because she was afraid of what they'd think of her past if they knew, but because of her refusal to take the responsibility of her job as a behavioral analyst?

How many times had she called herself a fraud? Too many to count. Was it because it was easier to think of herself as a fraud who got lucky with some of her analyses?

She'd certainly lived in fear the past four years of doing something majorly wrong and getting fired. Of getting fired for no reason at all.

Either way, maybe it was time to stop letting her feelings about the past control her every action. It had stunted her growth professionally, for sure. But it had also stopped her from making any friends.

From having any intimate contact with anyone at all.

All the stuff Brandon had said, she was going to have to sort through. It would take a while. Some of it wasn't correct, but some of it was dead-on.

Especially the part about not letting the past control her future anymore.

She'd hated seeing Harry today. Hated even worse

seeing the stuttering idiot she'd become around him. The same with her aunt and uncle in the car yesterday, afraid to face them.

These people were from her past and didn't have any control over her unless Andrea gave them that control.

She was tired of giving control over to anyone or anything else but herself. She'd lived without things she wanted—friendship, companionship—for too long. Let her fear convince her to give them up.

She wanted sex and she wanted it with Brandon Han.

She shot off from where she'd been sitting on her bed, the fading evening sun shining on her through the window. She was out the door and knocking on his before she could let herself overthink it too much.

"Hey," he said to her, his eyes traveling all over her face. "Are you okay? I was afraid I said too much, that I overstepped my bounds—"

Andrea grabbed his tie and pulled his mouth down to hers, stretching up on her toes to meet him. She didn't have far to go in her heels.

She thought for a second he might pull away, refuse, but he didn't. Instead he wrapped an arm around her waist and pulled her rapidly, fully, against him. He spun them around, getting her out of the doorway so he could shut it.

The heat was instantaneous. Overwhelming. It seemed to pool through her entire body. The fact that Brandon obviously felt it too just made the heat increase.

She'd wanted this man for years. She'd been afraid to show her attraction, to move on it, because of her past, of what he might find out.

But now he knew. And beyond that, damn her past and the hold it had had over her for so long.

He backed her up until she was against the wall, their bodies pressed so close against each other there was no room for anything else. Still, her hands gripped his waist, tugging him closer to her before sliding up his back to link behind his neck to capture him. The heat of his body against hers thawed something that had been frozen in her for far too long.

His lips were the perfect blend of firm and soft. Her eyes slid closed as his large hands came up to cup her face, to take control of the melding of their mouths. Andrea was glad to give over the control. She wanted him to give her whatever it took to ease the hunger that clawed at her every time she saw him.

Brandon kissed his way across her jaw and over to her ear. She couldn't stop the quiet gasp that escaped her when he bit gently on her lobe.

"Are you sure this is what you want, Andrea?" he whispered. She could feel his hot breath against her cheek.

More than anything else she'd ever wanted.

"Yes," she murmured, her eyes still closed, her arms sliding to his shoulders, trying to force his big body closer to hers.

But he held firm. "We can wait. It doesn't have to be tonight."

Her eyes flew open. Had she misread him? Did he really not want her? How could she have been so wrong about something like this?

"Is this not what you want?" She choked the words out.

"Oh, it is very much what I want." He stepped his body up against hers so there was no space between them whatsoever, leaving her no doubt that he did want her. "I'm just trying to be a gentleman."

"I don't want a gentleman. I want you."

He smiled. A wicked, hot smile that had her insides melting.

Then his mouth was instantly back on hers, the kiss harder, more urgent. He licked deep into her mouth and they both groaned. He slid his arm around her waist, pulling her off the wall, closer to his chest, so he could ease her blazer down her shoulders. He tossed it over on the small table where his also lay.

He brought his lips back to hers and began unbuttoning her blouse. "You cannot imagine how many times I've wanted to get you out of the perfectly professional suits you wear."

She smiled against his mouth. "I've had a few similar thoughts about you and those shirts and ties."

"Well, then." His brown eyes were so clear she couldn't look away. "I think we've delayed gratification long enough."

They made quick work of getting rid of the rest of their clothes.

He reached down and crooked an arm under her knees, swinging her up in his arms as though she didn't weigh anything at all and carrying her over to the bed. He laid her gently on it and reached down to devour her mouth again as if he couldn't bear to be away from her lips for another second.

A hot ache grew in her throat as his lips moved down

her jaw to her neck and bit gently; her fingers slid into his thick black hair. His lips grew more dominating as his hands moved downward, skimming either side of her body to her thighs and back up, before pulling her tightly to him in a raw act of possession.

He hoisted himself up onto his arms for a moment so he could look down at her body then back up to her face.

"Mine," he whispered fiercely, and she almost didn't recognize him as the controlled, intelligent being he usually was.

It ignited something inside her. A burning she knew only he could ease.

Andrea pulled him closer and forgot about the past, forgot about the future, forgot about everything but the heat and desire between them.

Chapter Eleven

He caught her trying to get back out of bed in the middle of the night. To sneak back to her room.

"Not this time," he murmured, reaching an arm out to hook her waist and pull her back into bed next to him. "No sneaking off."

"I should probably go back to my own room," she said.

"In the morning," he said, snuggling into her neck. "Sleep now."

He held her close, her back to his front, running a soothing hand slowly up to her shoulder, then back down, catching her waist then following the line of her body down to her hip and outer thigh, then back up again.

He wanted her to rest, to relax, to get the sleep she needed. Even before the mind-blowing sex they'd just had, it had already been a pretty overwhelming day. Hell, the whole week had been stressful for her.

The warrior in him wanted to protect her, to keep her in his arms until she got the rest—the peace— she needed. He wanted to hold her and keep her safe from anything that would harm her. But even more he wished he could go back and protect the girl she had been. The one who had been forced to work for the likes of Harry Minkley at Jaguar's just to survive. His teeth ground thinking about it—about her on a stage she hated with men leering at her—but he forced the hand that touched her to remain calm, soothing.

He soon realized she was not relaxing under his touch and definitely wasn't going to sleep.

"What's going on in that head of yours?" he asked against her hair.

"I've never slept with someone before. It's weird. I can't relax."

Brandon tensed. "What? You've never..." Had he heard her right?

"Well, I've...you know...had sex before. A couple times in high school. But it was a quickie and never in an actual bed. At night. Ugh."

She pulled the cover up over her head, embarrassed.

It made sense that she hadn't been with anyone since high school. She'd kept herself so apart from everyone else at Omega, there couldn't have been much chance to find someone she was attracted to.

It hurt him again to think of her alone for all those years. Especially when she hadn't needed to be.

He pulled her in closer to him and wrapped an arm around her waist. He slid his other arm under her pillow so her head rested on it.

"There's nothing to it. You just take a few deep breaths and let your eyes close."

"Sometimes I have nightmares."

"About what?"

"Mostly my uncle. That he is attacking me, hitting

me, before I can really get awake and away from him. That was finally the reason I left home. Because I knew eventually he would kill me."

"Somebody should've helped you. A school counselor, a doctor, somebody."

He felt her shrug against him. "I was good at being invisible. And terrible at asking for help."

"The trouble asking for help is still a problem, I see. You need to get better at that."

"Yeah, probably. I'm still pretty good at being invisible. I don't think anyone knows me around Omega."

Brandon laughed outright at that. She turned toward him. "What? I don't ever really talk to anyone."

"That doesn't mean they don't notice you, sweetheart. Most are just too scared to start up a conversation with you. You're known as being…" He cut himself off. He didn't want to hurt her feelings.

"What?"

"A loner. Not someone who wants to socialize with others."

"That's pretty much true, I guess."

"Not anymore. Not once we get back to Colorado Springs." He felt her stiffen. "But we don't have to talk about that right now. Right now you just practice the task at hand."

"Oh yeah? What's that?"

"Learning how to sleep with my arms around you."

"Okay, that I can do."

Brandon held her until he felt the tension ease out of her body and her breathing take on the deeper evenness of sleep. But it was a long time before he could sleep himself.

ANDREA STILL SNEAKED out a little before dawn. She wasn't trying to make Brandon angry. She wasn't even trying to get away from him. She just needed to be by herself. To regroup before seeing him again.

Before seeing his gorgeous brown eyes and striking cheekbones. His thick black hair she didn't know if she'd be able to stop her fingers from running through next time she saw him.

Everything about last night had been perfect. And she wasn't running now. Wasn't scared. Or at least wasn't scared of being close to Brandon. It was just that being close to him—being close to *anyone*—for that long was hard for her. She'd spent a lifetime keeping people at arm's length. That habit wasn't going to change overnight.

Not that Brandon had given any sort of indication that he was interested in anything more than just last night. She wished she had more experience with this sort of situation. She'd known one thing: if he'd awakened this morning and she'd sensed regret from him, it would've broken something inside her that couldn't be fixed.

So maybe she was running a little bit.

After putting on jeans and a shirt, for once not feeling the overwhelming need to look immaculately professional, she headed out to the hotel's small dining room as she had yesterday.

She was hungry. She and Brandon hadn't had much dinner and had expended considerable energy during the night. But first things first: coffee.

The lobby was deserted; she couldn't even see someone working behind the counter. The little dining room was also empty.

But for some reason Andrea felt like someone was watching her. She spun all the way around, but couldn't see anyone, just the shadows from the sun starting to rise behind the clouds. It cast an eerie light in the building.

But she could swear she could feel rage, violence, hatred pointed in her direction. She'd felt them enough from her uncle over the years to recognize the emotions.

Was her uncle here?

She was about to go back to her room, to lock herself in, but stopped. No. There wasn't any reason to be frightened. No reason to go hide somewhere.

There was no one here. Just her own imagination—coupled with not getting enough sleep—that was messing with her mind. This *town* messed with her mind.

And if her uncle and aunt were here, she would deal with it.

She forced herself to get the coffee she wanted, then sat down at the corner table. Her back was to a wall and she could see everything that happened in both the dining room and through the glass into the lobby.

She felt better a couple of minutes later when three guys came walking—albeit quite unsteadily—into the lobby. Maybe that was whose presence she had sensed, although it seemed unlikely. They were all laughing so hard she would be surprised if they didn't wake sleeping guests.

They'd obviously been out all night, were barely sober and were highly amused with themselves. They were college-aged, a little younger than Andrea. Clean-cut, good-looking guys.

"Top of the morning to you, miss," one of them said as the others made a beeline to the coffeepot.

Andrea raised an eyebrow. *Top of the morning?* These guys were definitely still drunk. Normally that would have made her tense, but, although she was wary, she found herself too relaxed after last night to jump back into full tension mode.

"Looks like you fellows had a good time. I'm hoping you didn't drive here just now."

"Oh no," another one said, holding up two fingers. "Scout's honor, we took a cab."

"But we do have to drive home in just a few hours." All of them groaned at that. "They're going to have to send security to drag us out of bed at checkout time."

The third one added a ton of sugar to his coffee and grabbed a Danish. "We've got to pace ourselves, you guys. We're never going to make it through the pilgrimage if we keep having nights like last night."

They all smiled. "But what a night."

"Pilgrimage?" Andrea shook her head. "I'm almost afraid to ask what pilgrimage you guys might be on that has left you in a state like this."

Guy number one eased himself into the table next to her, wincing at the sunlight beginning to come through the lobby windows.

"We went back to a place we heard about on the Devils and Angels Pilgrimage."

Andrea had no idea what that was.

"We go to Arizona State," he explained.

"The Sun Devils," Andrea said. Anyone from around here knew Arizona State's mascot.

"Yes!" The guys were all inordinately pleased that she knew that. They got distracted and started talking to each other about their school's latest basketball endeavors. Evidently the Sun Devils were doing well.

Andrea just went back to drinking her coffee; she wasn't interested in basketball statistics. Honestly, she wasn't interested in these guys at all, but knew they'd leave of their own accord soon.

Finally they remembered she was there and that they'd been in the middle of telling her something.

"Sorry. Anyway, Devils and Angels Pilgrimage. One of the local DJs decided he was going to travel all over Arizona to find the best…" The guy stopped, looking at Andrea, unsure how to continue.

He was embarrassed. Andrea could feel it radiate from him. One of the other guys leaned down and whispered something in his ear.

"The best exotic dance clubs," the first guy continued, obviously relieved to have found a more neutral phrase. "All over the state. Some fraternities are taking part in the pilgrimage, including ours."

"So, what, a different club each week?" she asked.

"Yep." He got a bent postcard out of his pocket and slid it to her. "See, we've done the first six and now have three more to go."

The postcard wasn't too difficult to read since it was just a list of clubs and dates on one side. A picture of a scantily clad she-devil and angel sitting on the shoulders of DJ Shawn "Shocker" Sheppard on the other.

But what caught Andrea's attention was three clubs

on the list. Three of their four dead girls had worked at three of them.

"Do you mind if I keep this?" she asked.

"Sure," the guy said, sitting up straighter and looking at her more carefully. "Hey, are you interested in going to any of the clubs with us? There are always a few women there, even straight ones. I'm Pete. We'd love to have you. It would be a lot of—"

"She's not interested, but thanks." Brandon's deep voice came from behind them. "Or if she is, I'll be the one to take her."

He slid into the chair next to Andrea, kissing her on the way down. "Good morning."

"Morning," she murmured against his lips. Brandon pulled back, but kept his arm around Andrea's chair. The message that she was off-limits was more than clear.

"Yeah, well, we've got to get some rest," the college guys said, instinctively backing away from the threat they could feel in Brandon. "The information on the postcard is also on the DJ's website. It's a whole big thing where people vote and they talk about it on the show. It's pretty wild."

The guys grabbed a few more things to eat and then headed up to their room. Pete winked at her over his shoulder and Andrea couldn't help but smile.

"Things are getting progressively worse with you," Brandon told her as he stood to get a cup of coffee. "Yesterday you sneak out of the bed. Today you sneak out of the bed and have three boyfriends by the time I get to breakfast."

"If it helps, I think only Petey wanted to be my boyfriend." She smiled, a little shocked at herself. She wasn't sure where this ability to make light flirtation was coming from, but it was pleasantly surprising.

Brandon turned and leaned against the counter, crossing his arms over his chest. "I might have to start handcuffing you to the bed so you don't escape."

She grinned. "I believe that would be improper use of your restraints, Agent Han."

The heat in his eyes caused her to blush. The thought of being handcuffed to Brandon's bed sent explosions throughout her body.

She liked knowing this man—with all his brains and degrees—wanted her.

He stood there for a long moment just looking at her. The heat in his eyes never went away, but a soft smile formed on his lips as he studied her.

"What?" she finally asked.

He came back to the table and sat across from her this time, leaning close. "You know, I've seen you in your suits, dressed impeccably professional, and totally naked. Nothing in between."

She felt her face burn. "Oh."

"So seeing you in jeans and a shirt is nice. Relaxed."

She leaned into him. "I feel nice. Relaxed."

And she did, amazingly. She didn't have to worry about her secrets being found out; Brandon already knew them. Even the earlier uneasiness about someone watching her had fled. She was here with him and she was relaxed.

She didn't know how long it would last, but for the moment she was willing to just enjoy it.

Chapter Twelve

"So, what did your boyfriend give you there?" Brandon asked between bites of his cereal.

A number of couples and families were around them now, the romantic mood that had engulfed them broken, but not the easiness.

"Something I wanted to check into. See if the dates lined up." She slid over the postcard with the dates the DJ would be visiting the different clubs. "I noticed they were at Jaguar's three nights ago and at Allure last week."

He took the card to study it. "And at Diamond Cabaret two weeks before that, which would be right around when the first victim was found."

"I know the dates don't correspond with their deaths, but I just thought it was interesting that it was the same order."

Brandon nodded. "Very interesting."

"Do you think this DJ Shawn Shocker has anything to do with it?"

"I doubt he is our culprit. Purity doesn't really look like his thing."

She looked at the back of the card with the picture

of the DJ and the angel and she-devil on his shoulders. No, Andrea wouldn't peg him as the killer, either. "So maybe it's someone, like Petey and his friends, traveling around on the 'pilgrimage' with DJ Shocker."

Brandon nodded. "Definitely a possibility. Actually, this could be the biggest break in the case we've had so far. Good job."

She smiled, then looked at the paper again. "It doesn't explain about victim number two, Ashley Judson. She didn't work at a dance club at all, one on or off DJ Shocker's list."

"You're right. But also, there was no one killed from the club that the DJ visited that week."

"What does that mean?"

Brandon shrugged, looking at his notebook. "Let's follow this thread all the way out." He lowered his voice so their conversation wouldn't be overheard by the few people eating breakfast. "Let's say it's a DJ Shocker groupie who's committing our crimes. Someone who is following Shocker from club to club, picking a woman and killing her a day or two later.

"Okay, victim number one, Yvette Tyler, was killed one day after Shocker's stop at Diamond Cabaret. There were no reported deaths after Shocker's stop at Vixen's the next week."

"But victim number two was killed where she worked at the truck stop."

Brandon nodded. "And we know she moonlighted as a prostitute."

"Shocker's group headed to Allure the following week. Noelle Brumby was found dead two days later." Andrea used sugar packets to provide a graphic representation of what she was saying. "And then Shocker was at Jaguar's on Tuesday and Jillian Spires was found yesterday, so killed Wednesday night."

Brandon stood. "Definitely fits. We need to get this to the sheriff's office."

SITTING IN OFFICER Kendrick's office two hours later, Andrea back in one of her professional suits, Brandon could feel frustration pooling all around him. They weren't going to get any help from the locals.

Kendrick had pretty much been ordered to let the case go and release it to the City of Phoenix homicide department. The Maricopa County Sheriff's Department had neither the resources nor the manpower to continue the investigation.

And honestly, except for Kendrick, Brandon wasn't sure they had much of a desire.

The conference call with Gerardo Jennison with the City of Phoenix PD hadn't offered much hope, either. They would offer their labs, coroners, crime-scene investigators and even continue to be a liaison, but they couldn't afford to put much detective and officer manpower on it. Phoenix and Maricopa County in general had bigger problems than the deaths of four women on their hands: they were dealing with unprecedented biker gang wars all along Interstate 10.

Unless something drastically changed, he and Andrea were on their own when it came to investigating. The sheriff's office promised to send out a notice to the owners of the exotic dance clubs in the area, asking them to warn the women working there to be extra cautious.

But that was it. No one else was working full-time on trying to find the killer.

He could feel Andrea becoming more agitated, so Brandon wrapped up the conference call and meeting pretty quickly. He'd been around red tape long enough to know that sometimes you just worked around it instead of trying to go through it. He led Andrea back out to the car.

"They don't care at all," she said, barely out the door. "The deaths of these women mean *nothing* to them."

He walked with her toward the parking lot, stopping by a tree that was at least a little bit away from the main entrance. "I know it seems that way, but I don't think that's true. Money and manpower are finite resources. The department wants to put them both where it's going to help the most number of people."

Andrea ran her fingers through her blond hair. Brandon had never seen her this aggravated before.

"If it wasn't for us, *nobody* would be looking into their deaths. Trying to figure out what happened. Trying to stop it from happening again."

He ran a hand up her arm. "The locals want to help, too. They just don't have the funds."

She turned away from him, looking off into the desert that surrounded them. "What if DJ Shocker had decided to do this stupid tour four years ago? I could've been the one the police found yesterday. And just like those four other women, nobody would've cared about my death. No family members would have stormed the sheriff's office demanding the killer be caught."

Although he knew it was probably the truth, everything in Brandon tightened in rejection at the thought.

The thought that she could've died without his ever knowing her.

"Andrea—"

"I care about these women, Brandon. I don't know them, but I care."

He turned her around and folded her into his arms, thankful that she didn't pull away. He needed to have her close to him right now, to know that she was okay.

"I know you do."

"I will stand for them. Find the killer. Stop this from happening to other women. No matter what choices they made in their lives, they didn't deserve to die like that."

"Together. We will stop this guy together."

He could feel her nod against his chest before she took a step back. "I have a plan."

"Okay."

"It involves us both stepping outside our comfort zones a little."

Brandon grimaced slightly. He wasn't sure he liked the sound of this. "Okay."

"We've got four days until DJ Shocker's next club appearance. We'll talk to him, talk to his production crew, see who the groupies are, following from club to club."

He nodded. "Okay, good. I already have an appointment lined up with him this afternoon."

"We'll need to interview those people. See what we can figure out from them."

Brandon nodded. "Yes." So far none of this was out of their comfort zone.

"We know that Club Paradise, on the northern side of Phoenix, is where the party is heading next." She took a deep breath, then continued in a rush. "I'll go undercover. Get a job there as a stripper. Try to lure the killer o—"

"No." The word was out of his mouth almost before his brain had processed what she was saying.

"Brandon, it's a good plan—"

"No."

He could feel the warrior inside him rising up and fought to keep hold of the logical, reasonable side of his mind.

There was no way in hell she was getting up on-stage naked in front of strangers and trying to lure out a killer.

No. And no.

He couldn't drag her away and lock her in a room to keep her safe—and away from prying eyes—so he fought to find the logical words to make his case.

"First of all, you're not a trained agent. You don't have the skills or experience to work undercover. Not to mention, what if the killer *does* come after you? You don't have the hand-to-hand or weapons defense training you need to protect yourself."

"But—"

"Not to mention, as someone who holds a doctorate in psychology, I cannot even begin to list the ways it would damage your psyche to go back into a situation like that. To put yourself back into the club scene where you were objectified by men could have a truly damaging effect on your state of mind."

Brandon began pacing back and forth.

"You're just beginning to come out of your proverbial shell, connect with other people—me in particular—and to place yourself back into the exact situation where you found such shame and—"

"Brandon."

"Fear will only set you back emotionally, which is not what…"

"Brandon." She said his name again, but this time she stepped in front of him and touched his cheek, stopping his pacing.

He stared down at her clear green eyes. There were no shadows in them now, as there had been so often in the past. No fear. Just determination.

"You're frightened for me. I can feel it."

He wanted to deny it, to argue that he was just being reasonable—especially if she couldn't seem to be—but he knew it was the truth.

He was terrified at the thought of her doing this. Of the damaging effects it could have on her on multiple levels.

"Thank you," she continued. "For caring enough to be scared for me."

"It's not a good idea for you." He put his forehead against hers. "It will hurt you in ways you're not really considering right now."

"I know it's not the best plan for me. But right now I need to think about whether it's the best plan for Jillian Spires and Noelle Brumby, and the other women who will come next if we don't stop this guy."

Brandon straightened. Objectively speaking, for the case and stopping the killer, it was actually a pretty good plan. But he still didn't like it one bit.

"But what about you not having training?"

"I was a stripper for a year and a half. I think I have all the training I need."

"No, law-enforcement training. Self-defense training."

"I have some. Drackett required me to have some."

Brandon planned to make sure she had more. Not just for this case, but because Andrea needed to know she could take care of herself, that she never had to be a victim again.

"*Some* is not enough in a situation like this. Especially when you're trying to capture the attention of a killer."

Brandon could feel another plan formulating in his brain. Within just a few seconds he had run a dozen pros and cons mentally and had come up with some plausible alternates to her plan.

"I need to do this, Brandon. It's the best way. You know that."

He held up a finger to get her to wait a moment more as everything fell into place in his mind.

"Fine. But you don't go undercover as one of the main performers. You go under as a waitress. One of our victims wasn't a dancer at all, so that can't be the only link. You'll be able to get up close with the patrons, especially when DJ Shocker is there. See if you can get any readings of anything unusual."

Andrea nodded slowly. "Okay."

"I will also be in the club at all times when you're there. I'll come in as a customer, but under no circumstances are you to leave with anyone except me."

"Okay, that's probably for the best."

"And I'm going to call Steve and tell him we need

out of the hotel and into a rental house. One that has a lot of space in the living room."

"Why?"

"Because if you're going to set yourself up as bait for a killer, I'm going to make damn certain you know more than just *some* defense tactics. We have four days. Anytime we're not interviewing suspects or investigating the case, you're going to find yourself going hand to hand with me."

Chapter Thirteen

"Can't you arrest him for something?" Andrea leaned over and muttered under her breath to Brandon. *"Anything?"*

They'd been in the lobby of DJ Shawn "Shocker" Sheppard's radio station for the past thirty minutes. Unfortunately, because DJ Shocker was doing a live show, they hadn't been able to question him yet. They'd also been forced to listen to his show.

Distasteful would be the most polite word for it. Less polite terms would be *vulgar, juvenile* and *ridiculous*.

"Unfortunately, being an idiot is not currently a crime in this country. So, no, I can't arrest him." Brandon looked as disgusted as she felt.

The radio program catered to college students—men in particular—and the humor was rowdy and raunchy. At least one word every second would have to be bleeped out over normal airways, although most of the audience was probably listening to the station over the internet, where no censoring was needed.

Andrea had listened for the past half hour, teeth grinding, as DJ Shocker had attempted to make a case for the banning of all women's sports bras. He'd used every obnoxious tactic from "that's how God would want it" to trying to compare the bras to illegal performance-enhancing drugs.

The entire premise was asinine, but that was the point. DJ Shocker wanted to live up to his name.

They could see him through the large window that separated the waiting room from the radio booth. DJ Shocker wasn't a bad-looking guy. Probably in his late thirties, way too old to be saying the ridiculous stuff he spewed. His show was on the air three hours a day, five days a week. And it was not only one of the most popular radio talk shows in Arizona, but a top-twenty across the whole country. People couldn't wait to hear what he would say next.

Andrea couldn't wait for him to shut up.

He finally did, tying in the topic du jour with his Devils and Angels pilgrimage tour. He invited every-one out to Club Paradise in four days. It would be the focus of much conversation in next week's shows, he promised. Not something any red-blooded Arizonian would want to miss.

The On Air sign finally flipped off. DJ Shocker was finished for the day. He took a moment to talk to his production crew, who'd gotten him through the past three hours. When an assistant came up to him and said something, pointing at Andrea and Brandon, he looked over.

"Hi. I'm Shawn Sheppard," DJ Shocker said as he walked out of the large radio booth, his voice sound-ing different than it had on air. "Megan told me you're law enforcement?"

"I'm Brandon Han." Brandon shook the hand the DJ

offered to him. "I'm with Omega Sector: Critical Response Division. This is Andrea Gordon."

Andrea shook his hand also, although she really didn't want to. At least he didn't come across quite so obnoxious in person. Although he was much shorter than she would've thought. Shorter than Andrea's five feet eight inches. *Much* shorter than Brandon's six feet.

"Has there been another threat against my life?"

Brandon looked over at Andrea. She hid a snicker in a cough. It was no surprise to her at all that someone would like to get rid of DJ Shocker permanently.

Brandon shook his head. "Not that we're aware of, Mr. Sheppard. Do you get a lot?"

The man shrugged. "Please, call me Shawn. I get a couple a year. Most of them we don't take seriously, although my lawyer has reported them all to the police."

Andrea watched him closely as he said it. He didn't seem to be hiding any fear about the threats.

"No, we're not here to talk about that. We'd like to ask you a few questions about the Angels and Devils Pilgrimage."

Shawn opened a bottle of water. "What about it?"

"Who came up with the idea for a strip-club tour?"

He answered as he led them down the hall toward his office. "My producers and I last summer. Something to do this winter where we could announce the best club around spring break—the end of March. College students make up my primary audience."

Andrea was content with letting Brandon ask the questions. She would just watch and try to gauge Shawn's feelings.

"Would you consider it a success so far?" Brandon asked, sitting in a chair next to Andrea. Shawn sat on a sofa.

"Yeah. Enough that we might do it again, or something similar, next year. The clubs seem to love it—I'm bringing in a lot of extra revenue for them. And I can't complain about the gig." He smiled at Andrea as he said it. She didn't smile back.

"Have you had any problems? Anything weird?"

The DJ's eyes narrowed slightly. "We've had a rowdy bunch sometimes. Once or twice it's gotten a little out of hand. A couple fights. A couple of guys getting a little too fresh with the dancers. Cops were called."

"Were any of these women involved with those situations?" Brandon laid out the pictures of the four victims, shots of them before they'd been killed so Shawn could see how they really would've looked. The DJ studied them.

He definitely recognized the first, Yvette Tyler. Andrea caught his slight change in breathing as well as a stiffening in his posture.

"What's this about?" Shawn asked. "Are these women suing me or something?"

"Do they have reason to sue you?" Brandon asked.

Shawn sat back and rolled his eyes. He was now aware that he was being accused of something here, rather than potentially being the victim as he had first thought. His posture became more defensive, less open.

"Have you heard my show? I offend everyone. I'm surprised there's not a lawsuit every week. Of course, I do have the First Amendment on my side."

"Do you recognize these women?"

"They're all dancers at the clubs, right? But I don't

know which was at which. It's all become a blur of pasties and pole dances."

Andrea pointed at Yvette's picture. "But you definitely know her, right?"

Shawn fidgeted. "Look, yeah. She was at one of the clubs a few weeks ago. Cute girl. Sexy. Great dancer. She cornered me in the hallway when I went to use the bathroom. Wanted to do some private dancing with me at home, if you know what I mean."

"And did you go home with her or vice versa?" Brandon asked.

"No. This was business for me. I was a celebrity. Leaving with her publicly wouldn't have been a good idea."

"What about leaving with her privately?"

"No. I didn't leave with her at all. She was irritated at the time, but when I saw her later after closing, she had moved on to some other guy. Was all over him at his car."

"Did that make you mad? Make you think she was some sort of slut or something?" Brandon asked.

"No. Honestly, I didn't care. I get a lot of women who throw themselves at me, if you know what I mean."

He glanced sideways at Andrea as if he expected her to do just that at any moment. She rolled her eyes.

"You're safe from me," Andrea said.

"What is this all really about? Not me going home with these women."

"No," Brandon said. "Unfortunately, all of these women are dead, Shawn."

"What?" He shot back against the sofa, eyes wide.

As far as Andrea could tell, the shock flowing off DJ

Shocker was completely authentic. He had not known the women were dead.

Brandon looked over at her and she gave him a slight nod. He nodded back, agreeing.

"When— What— How did they die?" Shawn looked back at the pictures.

"They were all murdered. Within a day or two of your Angels and Devils tour stopping at their place of business."

Shawn's face lost all color beneath his ginger hair. "Oh my God, are you serious? I'm sorry if I was flippant before. I had no idea they were dead. I swear I didn't have anything to do with this."

Brandon nodded. "We'll need your whereabouts at certain days and times, but we believe you. You're not actually a suspect, although at this time we're in the process of successfully eliminating as many people as possible."

"Okay." He buried his head in his hands. "Sure, sure. I'll provide you with whatever you need."

"Thank you."

Andrea leaned a little closer toward him. Now that he wasn't acting like a complete jerk, it wasn't so difficult. "Were there any people you remember seeing at all the clubs that showed a lot of interest in these women?"

"There's a number of guys, mostly from competing fraternities, that have come to most, if not all, of the tour stops."

"Do you remember anyone in particular?" Brandon asked.

Shawn thought about it for a long time. "No. I'm

sorry. The clubs are pretty crazy and I just wasn't paying attention. More focused on other things." He started to move back into sleazeball shocker mode, but stopped himself. "There were a lot of people around. A lot of women. A lot of guys. I don't remember anyone in particular. I'm sorry."

"Okay. Thanks for your assistance."

"Do we need to cancel the tour?"

"No. As a matter of fact, we think your tour is our best chance at catching the killer."

"Oh. Okay."

Brandon stood and Andrea followed suit.

"We're probably going to be at all your club appearances, from now on. We'd appreciate it if you didn't draw anyone's attention to us."

"Yeah, sure. Whatever will help."

Brandon shook Shawn's hand. The other man looked pretty shell-shocked. Andrea didn't blame him—it was a lot to take in. They left him and walked back out the way they'd come.

"He seemed pretty legitimately surprised," Brandon said, once they were outside.

"Yeah. I think he was definitely authentic about that. He's not our killer unless I'm way off."

"I agree."

They were almost to the car when Andrea turned back toward the building, sure that Shawn or someone from inside was calling them. But she didn't see anyone in the doorway.

But she knew someone was studying them.

"What's wrong?" Brandon asked, coming up behind her.

"Nothing. I don't know. I thought—" She looked around. That feeling from this morning was back. As if someone was watching her.

"What?" She felt Brandon's hand slide down the arm of her blazer. Having him near helped her shake it off. She was overtired. Had been bombarded by too much over the past few days.

Andrea shook off the feeling and leaned into Brandon. "Nothing. I thought I heard someone call me from back at the building. Must be the lack of sleep getting to me. You know any reasons why lack of sleep might have been a problem for me last night?"

Brandon smiled down at her. "Hmm. Maybe. Can't promise that won't happen again tonight."

Andrea hoped so. She would take a repeat of last night any way she could get it.

But there was a lot of work to do before either of them could think about sleeping—or not sleeping.

"We need to go back to Jaguar's so I can talk to the girls. See if they know or remember anything. Warn them to be careful."

"If the killer follows the pattern and keeps going with the tour, then the other women at Jaguar's should be safe," Brandon said.

"Well, we already have one discrepancy with the pattern. Victim number two wasn't a dancer at all. So I don't want to take any chances that the pattern gets changed and the killer comes back to Jaguar's."

He squeezed her shoulder. "Absolutely. Drackett is already making sure that the club owners are aware of the issue. He knows the local police department is also notifying them, but maybe hearing it from two different law-enforcement sources will make sure everyone is taking it seriously."

"Yeah, that's good."

"Are you sure you're okay?"

Andrea looked around again but didn't see anything that made her suspicious. The only thing she needed to be suspicious of was her tendency to see the boogeyman everywhere she looked.

Chapter Fourteen

At nine o'clock the next night Brandon was almost ready to exit his car and enter Club Paradise. Somehow he doubted very much that was what it would turn out to be.

Andrea was already inside, had been there for the past two hours working as a waitress. They'd cleared it with the club manager, "Big Mike," who'd been happy to keep the women who worked for him safe as well as have free help during the Saturday-night rush.

Big Mike, despite his name, was considerate and businesslike, the opposite of Harry Minkley at Jaguar's.

Brandon had been happy to spend a couple of hours putting the fear of God and law enforcement into Harry yesterday as Andrea talked to her friends.

Brandon hated the shadows that overtook Andrea's eyes whenever they were near Jaguar's. The shadows worsened around Harry. There were a number of scenarios Brandon could envision that would make Andrea react that way even four years later. None of them good.

So putting pressure on Harry, even though he wasn't really a viable suspect, was no hardship for Brandon. The man was sweating every corner he'd ever cut—and there were many—by the time Brandon left. Oh, and

Brandon said they would have constant surveillance on Harry and Jaguar's for at least the next year.

Brandon rolled his eyes at the thought of how much of a misuse of funds that would be, how ridiculously expensive, how it would never get approved. But Harry didn't need to know that. Every time someone came in looking slightly uptight, Harry would wonder if the person was undercover law enforcement. Good.

Brandon had watched Andrea interacting with the dancers of Jaguar's—some she'd known before, some she hadn't—and just kept his distance. The women, rightfully, had questions about Jillian Spires's death and Andrea answered them as best she could without giving away important details about the case. DJ Shocker was not mentioned by Andrea, although all the women said how crazy the night had been. Busy, especially for a Tuesday, not normally a great night. They'd all made a lot of money, which had made everyone happy.

None of them could remember any particular guy hanging around Jillian. Of course, there had been men everywhere because it was so busy.

Andrea warned them all to look out for each other. To walk to their cars at least in pairs. To carefully vet anyone new in their lives before trusting them. The women listened to Andrea in a way they never would've listened to Brandon. She was one of their own.

Keira, the woman Andrea had been so friendly with the day before, had come up to them after Andrea was finished and the other girls had left.

She told them that Jillian had been mentioning a new guy in her life. She hadn't given a name, just that it was

someone she'd known for a while and that their relationship had recently taken a turn toward the romantic.

It was something to look into and Brandon assured
her they would.

"Hey, you won't leave town without coming to say
goodbye, right?"

Keira had gorgeous wavy black hair that fell to the
middle of her back. She was shorter and more volup-
tuous than Andrea's tall slender build. The two of them
standing side by side made a striking pair.

"No, the case is far from over."

"Well, I want you to catch this sicko, but no just taking off like last time, okay?"

"I'm sorry, Keira. You were a good friend to me and
I shouldn't have done that." Andrea looked down, and
Brandon could see her begin to withdraw into herself.

Keira pulled Andrea to her in a huge hug. "Oh, honey,
once I found out you'd left with those two cops and you
weren't in any trouble, I was thrilled for you. This was
never the place you were meant to be."

Andrea wrapped her arms around Keira, also. "You
either, Kee. It's time to move on."

Keira slid back and winked at Andrea and smiled
over at Brandon. "It's not so bad for me. I know how
to work the stage, the whole place. But I got a plan,
don't you worry."

"I'm going to be moonlighting over at Club Paradise for the next few days," Andrea told her. "Undercover type stuff."

"Dancing?" Keira's eyes got big.

"No, just waiting tables. We've got reason to suspect the killer might target someone from there next."

"You be careful." She turned to Brandon. "You'll be there looking out for her?"

"Absolutely."

"Good. She's going to need it. She's all tough now, but she won't be feeling so tough when she's in the club. Even working the floor can be brutal. Sometimes more so with the wandering hands."

Brandon felt his own hands clench. The thought of drunk, sweaty men—of *any* men—pawing at Andrea had the warrior clawing to get out. He had to take a deep breath to calm himself.

Keira gave him a knowing smile. "Yeah, you're going to have to keep that under control if you want this undercover mission to work. She can handle it. She handled it for months when she worked here. Can you?"

Brandon hadn't known, still didn't know, as he was walking into the club now.

Club Paradise was nicer—more high-end—than Jaguar's, but in the end it was the same general principle: almost-naked women making themselves pseudo available.

These clubs sold a fantasy—a private dancer fantasy—where it didn't matter what a guy looked like, how short or tall, fat or skinny, skin tones or hairstyles: he got the girl.

For a price.

And only for a three-minute dance.

Although he'd been to a few for parties over the years, strip clubs had never been his thing. He had always found them to reek of desperation from both the men and women, although you could easily ignore it if you wanted to. And obviously many people wanted to.

A woman's naked body, although he could appreciate it, was not ultimately what turned him on. He found a woman's mind, her emotions, her ability to converse, infinitely more attractive.

Take Andrea, for instance. He couldn't deny he was attracted to her blond hair, green eyes, the delicate lines of her face. Her slender body, curved in just the right places, definitely turned him on.

But it was the other things: her obvious intelligence despite having to overcome her dyslexia, her shy smile, her ability at reading people. Those were the things that really attracted him to her.

The thumping sound of the music permeated the entire building. Brandon passed two bouncers who were actively surveilling the club, making sure none of the girls needed to be rescued from any of the men. Their job would get progressively more difficult as the night—and drinking—went on.

It was Saturday night, still relatively early for a place like this, but there were already men sitting around the main stage, where a dancer worked the pole with strength and skill that would rival an acrobat.

A topless acrobat, but still.

Big Mike had reserved a small table for Brandon in a strategic location in a corner near the bar. It wasn't the best seat if you wanted to be close to or watch the dancers, which was fine since Brandon didn't, but it was excellent for watching the rest of the club without looking as if he was doing so.

DJ Shocker's show would be here in three more days. Brandon and Andrea wanted to use her time working here leading up to that to try to identify regulars and people who could potentially pose a threat. Both so they knew who to watch and who they didn't really need to worry about watching when Tuesday rolled around.

Brandon would study behavior patterns: men who looked as though they were observing the girls with a more nefarious purpose in mind. Andrea would use her skills at reading body language and emotions to do the same thing, but from a stripper's point of view.

Sitting at his table, Brandon ordered a vodka tonic from a waitress who came by, smiling. He wouldn't drink it; he needed all his facilities firing at full speed, not dulled by alcohol. Next time around he'd switch it out for a club soda. It would look the same to anyone who happened to be observing.

He hadn't seen Andrea yet, but it was a big place. Big enough that he couldn't watch everything at one time. He had to constantly be looking around in order to see everyone, much like the bouncers. But he had to be much more subtle about it.

He wasn't wearing a suit, of course. Nobody in here was. He was wearing jeans and a black T-shirt, since he knew Club Paradise would just get warmer as the night went on and more bodies were packed inside.

His waitress brought his drink back, smiling, and Brandon paid, tipping generously. Drackett was not going to be thrilled when Brandon's Omega expense report included drinks from Club Paradise.

Brandon saw Andrea as she came out of a room from behind the bar. At first he could see only her shoulders and the side of her head through the crowd. Then a group of laughing guys moved and he could see her completely.

He picked up his drink and gulped it all the way down, alcohol be damned. If he'd had another he would've done the same thing.

This was Andrea as he'd never seen her, hell, would never even have been able to picture her in all her professional button-down suits.

Her shoulders were bare, her breasts cupped in a red corset bustier that cinched her already-small waist. Her black skirt was short, loose, not even reaching to midthigh. He couldn't tell what shoes she wore from where he sat, but knew from the way she towered over everyone that she had to be in heels.

Her hair that had always been perfectly tidy at work was now sexily, skillfully mussed. Her dark makeup gave her eyes a smoldering look.

Brandon wasn't the only one who noticed her. The group of guys that had parted so he could catch a glimpse of her soon saw the gorgeous waitress and made their way over to order more drinks. One put his hand on her waist; another played with a little piece of her hair.

Andrea laughed at something one of them said, then showed them to a table near the stage. All of them were staring at her legs as she walked away to get their order.

When her back was turned to them, one made a crude gesture to another, obviously about what he'd like to do to Andrea.

It took every ounce of willpower Brandon possessed to stay in his seat. What was he going to do, go punch some twentysomething guy in the face because he'd made a suggestive gesture?

Besides, look at what Andrea was wearing. Could he really blame the punk?

Brandon realized that was just as unfair a thought. Andrea was dressed the way all the waitresses here were dressed. It seemed to be a uniform of some sort: corset bustier and flirty skirts. All the girls had them on in different colors.

He hadn't even really noticed the outfit when his waitress had brought him his drink, but he sure as hell noticed it on Andrea.

He leaned back farther in his seat and forced his eyes away from her at the bar. He was here to study potential suspects, for anybody acting out of the ordinary. Not to act out of the ordinary himself.

But he couldn't stop himself from looking as Andrea brought the drinks back over to the guys. As she leaned down to put them on the table, all of their eyes flew to her breasts, hoping, he was sure, that there might be a happy accident with her top. One guy rubbed his hand up and down the back of her knee. Not going far enough up to be trouble, but certainly more intimate than he had a right to be.

Andrea just smiled and shook her head at him, as if scolding a toddler for being naughty. The men paid and she walked away. Their attention turned back to the stage.

Brandon sat back in his chair.

When he had found out a couple of days ago that Andrea had been a stripper, had worked at a place like this, Brandon had thought he was okay with it. He knew how quiet and reserved she was, plus the abuse that had occurred in her past, the desperate situation that had led her to it.

It had made for a very tragic figure in his mind.

What had he thought, that she had just cried all the way through every night she'd worked there? Sobbing and pushing away every man who came near her?

Obviously that hadn't happened. She'd worked the scenario to her advantage. Worked the men. She might have even enjoyed it all, if how she looked tonight—all smiles and flirtation—was anything to go by.

This jarring close-up of her scantily clad past made it a little harder for him to accept.

Brandon sat up and looked away from her again, from her laughs and flirtatiousness with seemingly every man in the room. The warrior snarled, demanding that he remove her from this situation, get her out of here. Prove—to all these men *and* her—she was his and only his.

But Brandon refused. His intellect ruled him, not his body and definitely not his emotions. Not the warrior. He had a job to do. He ignored the darkness that seemed to be waiting like a cavernous pit for him to fall into. And possibly never crawl back out.

No, he would do this job. Find and stop this killer.

Maybe Andrea wasn't the woman he'd thought. The partner, in more ways than one, that he'd been subconsciously hoping for. He'd survive.

Chapter Fifteen

"If a man comes up behind you and has you in a grasp you can't escape from, the most important thing is not to panic," Brandon had said yesterday evening as they went through self-defense moves in the large living room of the house Omega had rented for them for the rest of their stay here.

"Actually, not panicking is always the most important thing," he'd said, then continued to show her how to throw her arms up and then reach behind her attacker in a sweeping motion with her leg to take him down.

"It's not about size—you're never going to get attacked by someone smaller and weaker than you—it's about staying calm, focused and moving quickly."

It was some sort of jujitsu move, he'd told her. He had a black belt in it, as well as Tae Kwon Do. Andrea had always known about his intellectual prowess, but had no idea about the physical. Although she should've guessed after seeing his rock-hard abdomen and well-defined chest while in bed with him.

They'd practiced over and over, Brandon taking the brunt of the fall each time, until Andrea could do it naturally, without having to think about the different steps. Then they'd practiced more because Brandon said it needed to become muscle memory.

She'd finally stopped him by rolling on top of him after she'd swept him to the ground and kissing him.

"I don't think this is how you're going to want to behave during a crisis," he muttered against her lips, but she could feel his smile.

He'd slipped his arms under his head as she'd sat up, straddling his hips, and pulled her shirt over her head. She'd loved how his eyes had narrowed and his breath hissed out of his lips.

"I think I've got that particular attack crisis taken care of. There are some other one-on-one moves I'd like to work on now, if that's okay with you."

"Um…"

She reached back and unhooked her bra, throwing it to the side, and looked down at him, eyebrow arched. "Got any other moves we can commit to muscle memory?"

"I can definitely think of a couple."

Andrea held on to those memories of yesterday evening as the hours dragged on at Club Paradise. The memories of making love with Brandon with her on top, then in the shower, before he'd tenderly held her while they slept. She was getting used to having his arms around her, snuggling into him while sleeping.

She could use his strong arms around her now. It was nearly midnight, she had two more hours to work and the Saturday crowd was getting more rowdy.

Her first steps out the backstage door onto the club floor had brought back memories, all of them bad.

The feelings of being exposed, being watched, being thought of as a piece of meat.

The hands that touched her, sometimes innocently, sometimes much less so.

The bouncers were great here, much better than at Jaguar's. She'd already seen one step in at just a look from one of the waitresses. A guy who had pulled her down in his lap didn't want to let go. The bouncer made his way over, and without a word, he offered the waitress a hand to help her out of the guy's lap. He gave a pointed look to the man, again not saying a word. The guy had apologized to the waitress and everything had been fine.

Other waitresses, Andrea noticed, didn't mind the wandering hands of customers. Provided better tips. The bouncers seemed to know who was who.

Andrea still hated everything about it. Being down on the floor was almost worse than being up on the stage. At least onstage there was a distance—you were a performer. Here you were in the middle of the fray.

She'd seen Brandon sitting over at a corner table. She'd wanted to go over there, but didn't. She didn't want to encroach on another waitress's table, plus Brandon seemed to be deep in the study of the club. His face was pinched and focused, almost angry.

So, although she could desperately use a friendly smile from him, she forced herself to look away and do her job.

Survive this night, which had been her motto when working at Jaguar's, was not her job now. Now her job was doing what she could to find a killer.

It was difficult to get a reading of anyone in here.

It was too chaotic; her own feelings were too chaotic. Lust was the primary emotion, followed by guilt and greed. Alcohol caused everything to be hazy and people to have emotions they might not normally feel. She felt as if she was trying to filter through solid walls.

She tried to focus and find the emotions of anger, judgment, condescension. The ones the killer was most likely to have. It didn't take her long to realize the biggest place all three were coming from was Brandon's table.

She had to be wrong about that. Maybe Brandon was just using those emotions, channeling them almost, in order to try to find them in other people. Looking for nonverbal clues. She knew he wasn't the killer, but he definitely wasn't happy.

Andrea turned away from Brandon. She had to focus on what she was doing, not on how he seemed to be behaving.

Instead of trying to feel out general emotions for the whole place, Andrea decided to take it table by table.

She carried her drinks, trying to stay a little longer at each table to get a read on the men there.

The killer was icily controlled. What had been done to the women had not been done in a rage or burst of passion. It had been planned. The killer would study his victim. That was what Andrea was hoping to catch tonight. Someone who just didn't quite fit.

The emotions would be cold, not hot. Andrea needed to look beneath the heat of the lust and general rowdiness. She took a breath and centered herself.

The rest of the night went by more easily. She blocked everything from her mind besides trying to find the coldness of the killer. She thought of it in terms of color. Almost everything in the club was red and she was looking for blue.

Once she focused, the things that used to bother her so much when she worked at Jaguar's faded away. The hands that grasped at her leg or waist she ignored. She wasn't here to make tips; she was here to observe. She didn't need to flirt or smile in a suggestive manner. She froze them out and concentrated. These men were nothing to her. She could leave at any time.

She never found what she searched for. She wasn't able to pinpoint any source of contempt or cold calculation. Everything in here just seemed to be what someone would expect from a strip club: drunkenness, rowdiness and a lot of lust.

A little before 2:00 a.m. Big Mike yelled out for last call. Andrea made her way to the back room, taking her tips and splitting them among the other waitresses, slipping the money into their lockers. Her job was done for the night.

She was exhausted.

The last six hours had taken everything out of her. Getting past her fears, getting past the men, getting past it all and focusing despite her feelings. All for nothing.

She wanted Brandon. Wanted his arms around her. Wanted to go to their little house and leave this all behind her. At least until tomorrow night.

The plan was to exit separately so no one would think they were leaving together. Not that she thought anyone was watching her. But it never hurt to be sure.

Andrea stepped out the back employee door to discover it was storming. There were no windows inside Club Paradise, of course, and either the storm had just come up or Andrea had been so focused on finding who might be the killer that she hadn't even noticed if people had started coming in with wet hair. Either was possible.

She stood alone under the small awning covering the door, but it didn't offer much protection from the rain. Brandon should be here soon to get her. He would drive the car, even off the club parking lot if necessary, to make sure no one was watching him, then swing around to pick her up. She wasn't sure how long it would take.

She stood, huddled under the awning, trying to ward off the chill. The doorway was well lit, but the parking-lot lighting here in the back wasn't great, and beyond the lot seemed to be a vast darkness. She shivered.

That feeling was back. The feeling of someone watching her with anticipation and violence, but she was finally coming to realize that feeling was based on her physical exhaustion and emotional turmoil. Like her past, she wouldn't let it control her.

But she couldn't shake it.

She happened to be looking in the right direction—across the parking lot into the group of trees and cacti that surrounded the outer edge of Club Paradise—when the lightning struck.

She could see the outline of a man in the bright flash. Big, powerful. He wore a black rain jacket with a hood and the water flowed down it. Although the hood hid his features, she knew he was staring right at her.

This man intended to harm her. She had no doubt about it.

She immediately turned back to the door but found it locked. Damn it. Big Mike had told her they locked it from the inside after 9:00 p.m. to keep anyone from sneaking in that way. She rammed her fist against the door heavily, hoping the music was off and someone might hear her.

She turned back to where the man was. He was the killer. He had to be. She couldn't see anything in the darkness.

Was he almost on her? She strained her eyes but couldn't see anything. Dressed in black as he was, it would be difficult to see him in the lot. Lightning flashed again.

He was closer. Oh God, he was closer. He must be walking, taking his time. Which somehow panicked her even more. He was playing a game with her. Was that a knife in his hand?

She pounded again. Nothing. She was afraid to keep her back to him. What if he started to run and pounced?

Should she leave, try to make her way around to the front door? That would require running through some darkened parts of the parking lot around the edge of the building, but it seemed better than sitting here alone with her one jujitsu move and no one opening the door.

She turned, almost certain she would find the big man right behind her, but didn't. Her breath sawing in and out of her chest, Andrea jumped down the side of the small door ledge, keeping her back to the wall so the killer couldn't sneak up on her. She was about to run when she saw Brandon's car pulling around the corner.

It stopped, a beacon of safety standing between her

and whoever was out there in the darkness. When Brandon saw she was standing in the rain he got out.

"What's going on? Are you okay?"

"The k-killer." She could barely get the words out and pointed toward the lot where she'd seen the man. "I think he's out there. I saw him when lightning flashed."

Brandon immediately pulled out his weapon. "What? Are you sure?"

Andrea nodded, still trying to get in enough breath to calm her racing heart. "I know he was there."

"I'm going to check it out. You stay by the car."

"No!" There was no way she was letting him go alone, or staying here alone, for that matter. "I'll come with you."

"Andrea, you're not an agent—you don't need to do this."

"Yeah, well, I have a pair of eyes. I'm not letting you go out there with your back exposed."

Brandon nodded. "Fine. Let's drive the car that way so we at least have the headlights helping us."

They got in the car and he reached into the glove compartment, pulling out a gun. "This is a Glock 9 mm. Are you familiar with weapons at all?"

"Some, but only at the range."

"That's better than most." He handed it to her. "Just don't shoot me on accident."

They drove over near where Andrea had seen the man during the first flash of lightning. Brandon spun the car slowly in a semicircle to provide light on a wider area, but they didn't see anything.

"He seems to be gone now. Where did you see him?"

Andrea pointed. "At first it was over near those trees.

Then I was trying to get back inside and when I turned around again he was in the middle of the parking lot."

"That rain is coming down pretty hard out there, but let's see if we can find anything."

She didn't want to go. She wanted to stay inside the safety of the car. She wanted him to stay inside the safety of the car. She reached for his hand and was surprised when he pulled away as if she'd burned him.

She turned to him, but he didn't look at her.

"You can stay here if you want—that's okay."

She shook her head, not understanding exactly what was going on, the emotions that were radiating from him. Maybe, like inside the club, he was just focused. "No, I'll come, too."

They didn't find anything particularly useful. The rain was washing away everything too fast. Brandon did find two footprints right around where the man would've been watching her the first time she saw him. Brandon took a picture with his phone.

"There was definitely someone standing right here since the rain started. A perfect place to be watching the door when the women exited after work."

Andrea felt chilled to her very bones, as if she would never get warm again. The rain had both of them sopping wet, but the cold she felt came from the inside.

"He was coming for me, Brandon. I'm sure of it. I could feel him getting closer. I was about to make a run for the front door when you drove up." She managed to get the words out without her teeth chattering.

Brandon was only two feet away from her but he might as well have been a million miles. He finally turned and looked at her. She felt a slight softening from him before his walls rammed back up in place.

"Let's get you home."

ANDREA TOOK ONE look at herself in the bathroom mirror once they got home and understood some of the reason why Brandon was keeping such a distance. She looked like a drowned rat with too much makeup on.

The dark colors she'd used on her eyes to give herself more of a smoldering appearance at the club were now running down her cheeks. The carefully tousled hair now lay flat against her head in knots.

If she was Brandon she'd stay far away from her, also.

He was on the phone with Omega, or maybe the Phoenix police; Andrea wasn't sure which and really didn't care.

She definitely couldn't deny any longer that something had changed in Brandon since earlier this afternoon, when they'd made love for hours, and now, when he couldn't even seem to look at her.

It didn't take a genius to figure out what had happened. He'd seen her in her "natural" habitat. Had figured out what her life had really been like before. And it hadn't been pretty.

Andrea almost staggered under all the weight she could feel pressing down on her.

This was what she'd known from the beginning. Why she'd always tried to hide her past from everyone at Omega. Because ultimately it was ugly and seedy and lewd.

Brandon had thought he was okay with her past until

he'd come face-to-face with it tonight. Obviously, now he wasn't. He hadn't touched her once of his own accord since she left Club Paradise. She couldn't hide from that fact any longer.

He now found her distasteful.

She felt something deep inside her shatter at the thought. Pieces she knew she would never be able to put completely back together.

She couldn't bear to look at herself in the mirror any more. She stumbled over to the shower and turned it on. Once inside she found she didn't even have the strength to stand up. She just sat down and let the water pour all over her. She knew it would wash away the cold, the ruined makeup and the mud.

But it would never wash away her past.

Chapter Sixteen

The next morning Brandon was at a loss for what to do or say. It was new for him and not pleasant.

None of what he was feeling was pleasant.

Andrea sat quietly at the table, eating cereal. Was totally engrossed in her cereal as if she'd never eaten it before and it was the most fascinating thing she'd ever seen. Which he was sure had nothing to do with the cereal and everything to do with not having to talk to him.

Cold professionalism from them both.

By the time he had finished reporting the man Andrea had seen to the local police, she had been out of the shower and had enclosed herself in the smaller bedroom.

Not the one they'd slept in together the night before.

He told himself that was better, that they needed the space apart. That it would've been ugly if they'd had a confrontation right then. But part of him wanted to get it out in the open, fight it out.

Part of him wanted answers to how she could seem to enjoy dressing so scantily and flirting with dozens of unknown men all night.

The reasonable part of his brain nagged at him: Hadn't that been the plan? For her to blend in, do the job, get close enough to be able to read the emotions and nonverbal behavior of these men and see if any were acting out of place?

Just why the hell had she needed to seem to enjoy it so much?

Intellectually Brandon could see the unfairness of the direction of his thoughts. But the warrior couldn't. Couldn't seem to get past the short skirt and heels and hanging all over other men.

So he'd left her alone last night. Gotten hardly any sleep himself. And now they ate in silence.

She was dressed in her professional suit once more: pants, a cream-colored blouse and a blazer. Not a single hair was out of place, her makeup tame and tasteful.

But Brandon knew what lay beneath it.

Hell, just about any guy who'd been at Club Paradise last night had a pretty good idea of what lay beneath it.

He was struck again by the unfairness of his thoughts, but damned if he could stop them. He got up for another cup of coffee. He was going to need it to get through this day.

THE ICY PROFESSIONALISM and silence from both of them continued through the morning as they looked over the parking lot and surrounding area of Club Paradise. The local police had met them there to help search the wooded area, but besides a couple of footprints, nothing had come of it.

But standing where the man would've stood showed Brandon that he'd had an excellent view of the back door of the club. If it hadn't been for the lightning, Andrea might never have seen him at all. If he had kept to the shadows, he could've been on her before she'd even been aware of his presence.

It reminded Brandon once again that Andrea wasn't a trained agent and wouldn't be able to fight off an attacker. What he'd taught her hadn't nearly been enough. He needed to show her more, but that seemed highly unlikely given that they weren't even talking to each other at the moment.

They were now headed back to Jaguar's. Keira had called them; she'd found a note she was sure was in Jillian Spires's handwriting. It had some initials on it and part of a phone number.

Keira was waiting for them inside the empty club and gave Andrea a hug.

"How'd it go last night?"

Andrea rolled her eyes. "It was a Saturday night at a club. Some things haven't changed."

"Get any useful info?"

"No," Brandon said.

Keira stepped closer to Andrea, picking up on the tension between the two of them, touching her arm. "How are you doing? Was going back to it as hard as you thought?"

Andrea shuddered just the slightest bit. "Worse in some ways. But I had a job to do and that gave me something to focus on."

"You never should've gone back there." Keira angled her body so she was standing between Andrea and Brandon.

Brandon realized the shorter woman was trying to protect Andrea.

From him.

The thought was preposterous. Why would Andrea need protection from him?

Andrea's smile was soft and gentle as she looked at her friend. "I won't lie. It brought back a lot of the old memories and old fears. But at least I didn't have to call you to come bail me out this time."

Keira hugged Andrea tightly to her, almost motherly. "Well, you know I would have."

Brandon didn't know what the two women were talking about, but he could feel a weight beginning to sit in his chest. Looking at Andrea now with Keira, he realized the icy professionalism she'd had with him since they'd awakened this morning wasn't actually her true feeling. There was pain in her eyes, in her voice, in her posture that he'd missed before.

Missed because it hadn't been there or missed because he'd been too busy with his righteous anger to see it?

All he knew was right now Andrea definitely wasn't the same confidently flirtatious woman who used her body to get what she wanted that he'd seen with the men last night. Nor was she the consummate professional who'd greeted him coldly this morning, then went about her business.

Right now she just looked young. Haunted. Clutching a friendly hand because she desperately needed someone to hold on to.

The weight in his chest got a little heavier.

"But anyway, I got through it," Andrea told Keira.

Neither of them were looking at him. "We didn't really gather any useful intel, but hopefully now I should be more ready for tonight and especially tomorrow when DJ Shocker is there. That's what's important."

"You don't have to do it, you know," Keira whispered. "I'll come do it."

Andrea hugged the woman. "Thanks for the offer. But I can't teach you how to read people the way I can. It's just something that clicks in my brain."

Keira shrugged a delicate shoulder. "Okay. Let me know if you change your mind."

"So what did you find of Jillian Spires's?" Brandon asked.

Keira turned so her back wasn't to him and he could be included in the conversation. But he noticed her eyes were neither warm nor friendly when she looked at him, the way they were when she looked at Andrea.

"A note from last week. Evidently someone had given it to her and she had stuffed it in the drawer by the server's station."

"Why would she do that?" Brandon asked.

Keira rolled her eyes. "Our outfits—even when waiting tables—don't tend to have a lot of pockets or places to stuff paper."

"What did it say?" Andrea asked.

Keira walked a few steps to the bar where she'd placed a napkin that had been folded. "Here."

She handed it to Andrea, but Andrea looked at it briefly and handed it to Brandon, looking embarrassed. "It will take me too long to decipher that."

Because of the handwriting and water stains, the note would be hard for anyone to read, dyslexic or not, but Brandon couldn't find a way to reassure Andrea of that.

Trust me, I can give you a lot more thrills than DJ Shocker ever could. Text me when you get off work tonight. J

It had a phone number, but the last four numbers were unreadable because of liquid that had hit the napkin.

"That was given to Jillian the night DJ Shocker was here," Andrea said.

"Or maybe the night after," Brandon agreed. "Either way, this person would fit our MO. We know he was here for the DJ Shocker show and we know he wanted her attention."

"Will the phone number help?" Andrea asked. "The area code is local for Phoenix."

Brandon nodded. "It gives us something. We'll also get the police department to run this napkin for any forensic evidence, although at this point it's highly doubtful."

"Do you remember her with anyone, Keira?" Andrea asked softly.

"No. I'm sorry. The night with DJ Shocker was crazy. There were a ton of locals here, plus people we'd never seen before." Keira's distress was obvious.

"It's okay, Kee. You can't keep track of everything and watch over everyone. Even though you try." Andrea wrapped an arm around her.

"She was a nice kid." Keira shook her head. "Wasn't shy, like you. She was outgoing. Didn't mind flaunting what the good Lord gave her, if you know what I mean. Even down here waiting tables, she still had a lot of sass. And tended to go home with men from the club, even though we all warned her that was a bad idea."

"Everybody has to go their own way, Keira. You can't be mother to us all."

Keira, of course, wasn't old enough to be mother to any of these girls, was hardly old enough to be mother to a baby. But age had nothing to do with mothering instincts.

Keira gave them a crooked half smile. "I always try."

It was getting late in the afternoon. Andrea said her goodbyes to Keira, both of them needing time to get ready for the night's work. He left them so they could talk privately.

The thought brought the weight back to Brandon's chest. Everything he'd heard from Keira about Andrea did not mesh with the conclusions he'd drawn for himself after seeing her last night.

Maybe he needed to talk to her, to clear the air. To tell her what he was feeling.

Hey, I didn't like that you pranced around for a bunch of men while being so scantily clad last night. I know you were undercover but you didn't have to look like you were so comfortable with it.

Yeah, he didn't come across as a jackass with that thought. The weight in his chest got heavier.

"You ready?" she asked, joining him at the door. He turned and stared down at her.

"What?" she finally asked.

"Nothing. I—" Not knowing what to say, he stopped

himself and held the door open for her. Should he try to explain?

He was about to try as they walked outside, even knowing that it probably wouldn't come across well. But she stopped abruptly just a few feet out into the parking lot.

"What's wrong?" he asked, about to reach for his weapon.

"It's my—" She cleared her throat and started again. "It's my aunt. I don't see my uncle."

Brandon took his hand off his sidearm, but didn't relax his guard. He saw the older woman now. She was standing next to the same car that had been parked in front of the hotel on Tuesday.

Despite any coldness between him and Andrea, Brandon knew he would protect her from this.

"You don't have to talk to her," he told her, stepping closer. "We can just leave. Or I'll go talk to her if you want."

He could see the tension outlining Andrea's body. "No, like you said, they can't hurt me anymore. I don't know what she wants."

As Andrea walked toward her aunt, Brandon stayed close to her side. The older woman took a few steps toward them as they got closer to the vehicle. Andrea stopped about ten feet away.

"Hello, Margaret."

No title or anything to insinuate they were family.

"Andrea. You look so beautiful." The older woman moved closer but stopped when Andrea visibly flinched. "So grown-up."

"I have grown up since I was seventeen and left your house in the middle of the night, scared for my life."

It was Margaret's turn to flinch. "Andrea, I'm—"

"Where's Marlon?"

"Your uncle passed away two years ago."

Andrea nodded, obviously not curious how Marlon had died. She relaxed just the slightest bit. That man truly could never hurt her again.

"I don't expect you to forgive me for not stopping him from hurting you. But I am sorry. Sorry I wasn't stronger and didn't stand up to him."

Andrea nodded again. "Thank you for coming by."

Andrea began to walk away but her aunt stopped her.

"One of the ladies from church told me you were in town and working for law enforcement. She said you knew some people here."

Margaret just stared at the building for a moment. He wondered if she knew Andrea used to work there.

The older woman brought her gaze back to Andrea. "I knew I needed to come and make my apology face-to-face while I could. I didn't think you'd talk to me on the phone."

Everything about Andrea's stance clearly said her aunt was right.

"Well, it was nice of you to make the gesture." Andrea turned to their car, obviously finished with the conversation.

Her aunt reached out. "I also have a box of your things. Letters you received and a few items that were in your room that you left behind." She opened the door to the backseat of her car and took out a box that wasn't much bigger than a shoe box. "You used to like horses and collected a couple figurines."

Andrea stopped and turned back to her aunt, her eyes narrowing. "Yes, I remember those."

"They're in here. Please, honey, I know you don't want anything to do with me, but I wanted you to have these things."

Andrea hesitated for a moment, but then walked over to her aunt. When she reached out to take the box, Margaret put her hands over Andrea's.

"I stopped drinking. Marlon did too a few months before he died. Both of us realized what damage we'd done to you, and I'm so, so sorry. I know we'll never be family again, but I hope someday you'll be able to forgive me."

Andrea nodded again, but didn't say anything. Margaret held her hands so long Brandon took a step closer in case he needed to force Margaret to let go. Brandon's action caught Andrea's attention and seemed to pull her out of whatever place in the past she'd gone.

"Thank you for getting these to me." She gestured to the box while stepping backward, breaking the contact with her aunt.

"I'm so glad you've done so well for yourself," Margaret whispered. "That you were able to overcome everything and rise above it."

Andrea looked at her aunt, then at Brandon. "I'm learning that the people who hurt you are ultimately the ones who make you stronger."

Chapter Seventeen

The people who hurt you are ultimately the ones who make you stronger.

Andrea's words still rang clearly through his head hours later when he sat at the corner table of Club Paradise again.

He and Andrea had left her aunt, returned to the house, and Andrea had gone into her small room. She hadn't said anything to him besides the most basic of answers to his questions about food and particulars of the case. He'd left her at the house to take the napkin Keira had found to the locals for analysis.

When he'd come back Andrea had still been in her room, although there had been evidence that she'd fixed herself dinner. The box her aunt had given her lay unopened on the kitchen table.

They still hadn't said anything but polite phrases to each other as he took her to Club Paradise to get ready for her shift.

The weight in his chest hadn't gotten any less heavy, either.

She'd looked right at him when she'd said the words:

the people who hurt you are ultimately the ones who make you stronger.

It was now nearly eleven o'clock and he'd been watching the men in the club—watching Andrea— for more than an hour and a half from the same table as last night.

Despite the weight in his chest, he still couldn't stop his anger, his distaste, at seeing her flirt so easily with the men. At seeing her dressed so skimpily again, at knowing *others* were seeing her show off so much skin.

"How you doing there, Agent?"

Brandon's eyes flew to the petite form, dressed in high heels, jeans and a tank top, who plopped down in the chair across from him.

Keira.

Brandon sat back. "Hi. Didn't expect to see you here."

"Thought I'd come out, give a little support to our girl. I know she needs it."

Brandon looked over to where Andrea had crouched down near a low chair so a man in his midforties could give her his order. He noticed the man never took his eyes off her breasts cupped in the bustier. Andrea didn't seem to mind at all that the guy was salivating.

"She seems to be doing just fine on her own," Brandon said to Keira.

Keira's eyes narrowed, but she didn't say anything. A waitress, with *Kimmie* on her name tag, came over to take her order, and when she brought the drink back, Keira took a twenty-dollar bill, rolled it up and stuck it between the other woman's breasts—also visible from the bustier she wore. Keira winked at the waitress and she winked back.

"You into girls?" Brandon asked.

"No. Not that way." She took a sip of her drink. "Just like to support my sisters who work damn hard for their money then a lot of times are rushing to a second job or a family or something else that also requires their time."

Brandon hadn't necessarily thought about it like that, but guessed it could be true.

"Let's take our waitress, Kimmie. She's Andrea's age or a little younger. Maybe twenty-one."

Brandon nodded. "Probably."

"Maybe Kimmie got knocked up by someone who took off. Or has a husband who can't get a job. Or hell, maybe she's always dreamed of being a stripper. Whichever. She finds a job here. Any of that make you think less of her?"

"Not really."

"She comes in every night, smiles at all the guys. It's not hard for the good-looking frat-boy types. Maybe a little more difficult for the old ones or fat ones or ones that sneer at her. But she still does it, because, well, that's how you make a living at this job. Think less of Kimmie now?"

Brandon knew where Keira was going with this, but didn't stop her. "No, I don't think less of her."

"She gets up onstage and takes her clothes off and smiles. She works down on the floor serving drinks and smiles. She smiles. Because this is her job. Giving men something to look at is her job. And she does it well."

Brandon held a hand out in surrender, but Keira continued.

"There are some girls who have to use drugs in order to do it. Kimmie isn't one of those. There are some girls who make some extra money by going out in back and having sex with guys. But Kimmie doesn't do that, either. Because Kimmie's just trying to live—support her family or whatever—off the money she makes at this job. She doesn't give guys come-ons. Doesn't tease them. She just dresses up her admittedly beautiful body in a somewhat revealing outfit and smiles. Nothing more."

Brandon looked over at Andrea. She was smiling. But she wasn't touching any of the men, leading them on in any way. Like Kimmie, she was just doing her job.

Keira leaned over the table toward Brandon. "You got a problem with what Andrea's doing here tonight? What she did four years ago?"

Brandon shrugged. "I didn't think so until I saw her up close and in action. It's hard to watch. Hard to accept."

"Whose hang-up is it?" She gestured toward Andrea. "That sweet girl right there? I don't think so."

Keira took another sip of her drink. "Do you know why she was so popular onstage? Because everyone could tell she didn't really want to be there. Made her seem untouchable yet available at the same time. Guys ate it up."

Brandon shook his head. He didn't want to think about Andrea onstage, and thinking about her being up there when she didn't want to be was even worse, but Keira wouldn't relent.

"You see me? I am what I am. I go up onstage and I'm confident and strong and hot. It's not every guy's thing, but it's enough that I'm pretty popular. Do you think you could make me feel bad about myself?"

Brandon began to answer but she stopped him.

"Let me help you—no. Nothing you could say to me about my chosen profession would make me feel bad about myself. Because I am how I dance—confident and strong. I own my choices and I don't second-guess myself."

Brandon raised his glass in a sort of salute. Everything Keira said was obviously true.

"But you know what I'm not, Dr. Han? It is doctor, right?"

"Not medical, but PhD, yes."

"I'm not kind. I'm not willing to put myself on the line to help other people. I'm not willing to fight through hardships and claw my way up from the holes life tries to throw me in."

"I'm not sure life would be able to throw you in a hole." And he didn't think the other part was true, either.

She shrugged a delicate shoulder and glared at him. "One thing I know—I sure as hell wouldn't be willing to go back and do something that sickened me about myself, that broke my own heart, because it might help a complete stranger."

She pointed across the club where Andrea was talking to another group of men. "But I think we both know someone who did. Who *is*."

Brandon stared at Andrea for a long time. Finally Keira stood up, her drink empty. "It's time for me to get going. I have responsibilities having to do with stuff not here."

"I'll walk you out."

She put a hand out. "I'll be fine."

She walked a few steps before turning back to his table. "I don't know Andrea well. She doesn't let anybody know her well because she's afraid they'll hurt her. But I've seen the way she looks at you. She respects you, has opened herself to you."

Brandon couldn't deny that. Andrea had opened herself to him, in more ways than one.

"Knowing you were here had to make this even harder for her. That you might judge her. Hurt her like other people had. And then you did."

Brandon couldn't deny it. Keira was right.

She continued. "Andrea will eventually come to terms with the fact that she was a stripper. In the greater scheme of things, who the hell cares? It's in her past and it got her through. Someday she'll look back on her past and realize she has nothing to be ashamed of. I doubt when you look back at how you've treated her that you'll be able to realize the same."

HAVING THE FACT that you were a hypocritical jackass pointed out with such crystal clarity was pretty painful.

The image of Andrea, smiling and flirting with other

men in a skimpy outfit, seeming to enjoy it? It burned into his mind.

Another image tried to fight its way in, one of Andrea in the rain, cold, needing him. But he pushed it out.

He could admit to himself it was easier to deal with anger and disgust over stripper Andrea than with the feelings that swamped him over kind, talented, reserved Andrea.

Those feelings scared the hell out of him.

And it wasn't as if he'd said anything to Andrea about how seeing her at the club had made him feel. He wasn't that much of a jackass.

She was in the shower now. It was nearly 3:00 a.m. He was listening to a message left for him by Gerardo Jennison at the Phoenix police department with a report of what they'd found in the woods around Club Paradise today. It hadn't been much.

He sat down on the couch, realizing he'd been pacing. He pushed all thoughts of Andrea away and concentrated instead on the man she'd seen in the storm.

There'd been no sign of him tonight, and neither Brandon nor Andrea had found any persons of interest in the club. If the storm guy was the same one who had killed the other women then his MO seemed to be changing. He wasn't waiting until DJ Shocker's visits to pick his victims; he was hunting before.

Of course, he'd also killed Ashley Judson, victim number two. She hadn't been a stripper at all, just a waitress, although she'd had a reputation for serving up herself for truckers who stopped at her restaurant and were willing to pay the right price. That could certainly seem just as "impure" as the other women, who took their clothes off to make money.

But coming after Andrea didn't really make sense, since it was her first night and she hadn't really done anything "impure," unless the actual women he killed didn't matter, just someone who worked at a strip club.

Brandon sat back and let his mind work, doing what he did best, thinking of all the possibilities. Maybe the storm guy wasn't the serial killer at all. Maybe it was Damian Freihof. Brandon took out his phone and speed-dialed Steve.

"Damn it, Han, do you know it's three o'clock in the morning?" Steve asked by way of greeting.

"Sorry, boss. We've had a slight update." He explained the situation and what had happened to Andrea.

"Do you think the killer has turned his sights on her?" All traces of sleep were now gone from his boss's voice.

"Not unless he's changed his MO. I was wondering what the latest update on Damian Freihof was."

"It's still an active manhunt, but he was last seen near Midland, Texas."

"That's not out of the realm of possibility for arrival in Arizona."

"True. But it's also a direct route to Mexico, which is a logical place for him to be headed if he wants to get to South America. Plus, we still don't have any reason to think he'll actually come after Andrea. He hasn't had any contact with her since she's been at Omega."

"All right. Sorry to wake you. Keep me posted if anything changes."

"You'll be my first call. How has the undercover work been going?"

"Fine. Andrea jumped back into it like she'd never left. Seems like wearing next to nothing and flirting with total strangers is second nature to her."

There was a long silence on the other end.

"What?" Brandon finally asked.

"You're telling me that Andrea looked like she was having a good time while working at the club?"

"Yeah. She was fine. Happy, even. Why?"

"I must have misunderstood the nature of the club you were infiltrating. This club must be different than Jaguar's, more like a restaurant."

Brandon all but sneered. "No. It was a strip joint. Maybe a little higher rent than Jaguar's, but there were still mostly naked girls dancing on the stage. And the waitresses' outfits weren't much better. Drunken guys. Groping. You know the drill."

"And Andrea was all right?"

"More than. I'll bet she made a killing in tips. Looked perfectly at home in a bustier and heels. All smiles."

Brandon couldn't get the image out of his mind. It wasn't even the outfit that bothered him so much. He'd gladly have watched her all day in that skirt and top. Would've loved to have peeled her out of it. Under much different circumstances.

It was her actions. Her flirtations, friendliness. The smiles she'd given other men. Touches she'd allowed.

He felt the warrior clawing his way up. He wanted to go and beat down all the men who had dared to touch her. Then pin her to his side and make love to her until she was never even tempted to smile at another man.

Steve interrupted his thoughts. "Wow. She must be

better at undercover work than I would've thought. Good for her, for fighting through it to do her job."

"She didn't look like she was doing a job."

"Brandon, if you could've seen her at Jaguar's when Grace Parker and I picked her up there four years ago, you'd be amazed that she could even function tonight, much less do her undercover work well."

"What do you mean?"

"She was all but broken. She hated every minute she worked in that club—it was destroying her piece by piece. Going back into a similar situation has to be overwhelming for her, probably terrifying."

Brandon could feel something clench in the pit of his stomach. Again.

"I'm proud of her for just facing it," Steve continued. "Even if she had only made it for ten minutes, I still would've been proud. To hear that she did so well? Be sure to pass along my official and personal congratulations for a job well done."

Brandon murmured something; he wasn't quite sure what.

"I hope this will help you guys find the killer. Because I'm sure Andrea paid a high personal price getting out there the last two nights."

Brandon managed to say the correct words and end the call with his boss.

That feeling in his gut still hadn't gone away. Still felt like a heaviness pressing down on him. How heavy was the weight?

The exact weight of a judgmental, hypocritical ass.

Someone who had acted completely unprofessional the past two nights and it hadn't been the unseasoned consultant with no undercover experience. She'd done what she was supposed to do. Make nice with the locals and try to get a reading on anybody who might not fit in.

All Brandon had been able to see was the short skirt, revealing top and sexy makeup. Not the capable law-enforcement figure underneath.

Or the very vulnerable woman who had probably needed support from him. Possibly during her time at the club. Definitely afterward.

He'd turned away. Deliberately.

The shower had long since turned off. He realized Andrea hadn't come through the living room at all. Not that he expected her to come say good-night, but she hadn't come to get any food from the kitchen or even a glass of water.

Regardless of her outfit, she'd worked very hard for the five hours he'd watched and some time before he'd arrived. That tray probably would've gotten heavy after a while, and her heels were even higher than usual. That couldn't have been easy on her feet.

Brandon rubbed a hand down his face. She had preferred going to bed hungry and thirsty than to walk by him to get what she needed.

He headed back to one of the two bedrooms this house contained, looking at the one he and Andrea had slept in together two nights ago. They'd fallen in bed after showering, both exhausted by the hours of training and lovemaking. She'd slept in his arms the entire night, and he'd smiled when he'd awakened to still find her there. No running away this time.

But she wasn't in that bed now. It was empty, covers of the king-size bed still undisturbed. He walked over to the other, smaller room that barely fit the single bed, dresser and desk.

There was Andrea sound asleep.

The light in her room was on. Her back was pressed all the way against the wall the bed sat against, one arm resting halfway over her head in a defensive position. Even in sleep she was prepared for someone to strike.

Brandon knew he had added to her psychological need for that posture by his actions. The thought shredded him.

He pulled out the chair from the desk and sat in it, watching her sleep. He wanted to wake her up, to apologize.

He hadn't said anything that an outsider would consider cruel. Hadn't done anything that would seem unforgivable. But Brandon knew how sensitive Andrea was, the emotions she could sense and decipher. She'd known how he felt. His disapproval, his anger. The distaste he'd felt.

God, he would take it all back if he could.

Given some time to process it now, and with the help of both Keira and Steve, he realized he hadn't really been prepared to see her like that. Hadn't really come to grips that she had taken off her clothes for money when she was younger.

But now, sitting here, watching her, he realized he had no right to judge her. He'd been raised by two loving parents, surrounded by two brothers and a sister. He'd been a challenging child, acting out in his younger grades, on a route to trouble. His parents had loved him enough, known him well enough to realize the problem was he wasn't being challenged sufficiently. They'd moved him to a gifted academy, one that allowed him to excel at his own pace.

The course of his life had been set. He'd flourished from there.

Who'd been around to see that Andrea flourished? No one. The opposite, in fact.

She shouldn't have to apologize for how she had chosen to survive. The important fact was that she had. She was already ashamed of it.

He had added to that shame. What did that make him?

He reached toward her to wake her up, tell her all these things, beg her forgiveness, but dark circles under her eyes stopped him. She needed rest. She'd been working hard for days and hadn't been getting enough sleep. The things he needed to say could be said in the morning. They were his burden to carry.

He wanted to at least pick her up and carry her to the bed they'd shared. He wanted to hold her during the night. Be close to her.

But he had to face the fact that she might not want that anymore. She was sleeping peacefully now. For once he would make an unselfish decision concerning her and leave her alone.

She'd scrubbed her face completely clean, making her look so young and innocent and vulnerable that it was almost painful to look at her.

He realized she was exactly those things. Even when she had on a skimpy outfit and a ton of makeup and platform heels, she was still those things: young and innocent and vulnerable.

She had to go back there again tomorrow night—hell, it was so late, it was tonight—but this time he planned to make sure she understood that she wouldn't be going in there alone.

If there was one benefit of having an IQ as high as his, it was that you learned from your mistakes and you learned *fast*.

Chapter Eighteen

Andrea slept later than she had been, but not enough to wipe the exhaustion from her body. Her sleep had been plagued by nightmares. First ones that hadn't bothered her for a while, of her uncle and her life in Buckeye. Then ones of the past two nights, groping hands and the man she'd seen in the lightning.

Her heart began to thud just thinking about him.

She forced the thought of it out of her head. She had to admit she'd been so emotionally piqued getting off work in the storm that it was possible she'd imagined the whole thing. Not the man. She had definitely seen the man. But maybe he hadn't meant her any ill intent at all. Maybe he'd just been a guy walking across the parking lot and it just got all spooky-out-of-proportion because of the lightning.

She also didn't want to think about Brandon and how he obviously now felt about her. She noticed he'd left her where she was for the second night in a row, sleeping alone in the small guest bed. He hadn't wanted to be near her. Hadn't touched her at all since he'd seen her at Club Paradise.

She threw off her covers and got out of bed, still

fully dressed in sweatpants and a T-shirt. She even had a bra on. She knew sleeping fully clothed was something she did when she felt nervous or uncomfortable. A habit from the days when she'd had to run in the middle of the night from her uncle. Sometimes she fought the urge. Last night she hadn't.

She was surprised to see Brandon already awake, pulling out the beginnings of breakfast in the kitchen. She stopped in the doorway.

"Hi." His black hair was tousled and his chest was bare. Andrea fought the urge to lick her lips. It was totally unfair that she was this attracted to him when he obviously wasn't attracted to her lately.

"Want some coffee?" She nodded and he smiled at her before turning to get a mug and pour her some.

Her fingers touched his when he handed her the mug. At least this time he didn't jerk away as if he couldn't stand to touch her.

"Thanks." Her voice was husky with sleep. She didn't know what else to say to him.

"I'm going to make some breakfast, okay? I don't think you ate anything last night and you worked pretty hard." He smiled again. "Then we can compare notes, see if we come up with anything."

Andrea was confused by his behavior. This was different from the cold and distant Brandon she'd experienced for the past day and a half.

He was being professional, she realized, something in her sinking. He knew they still had to work together even though he found her distasteful. Their personal relationship was over but he was at least making an effort to make the situation less awkward. She could do the same.

It wasn't the first time she'd put back together the shattered pieces of her emotions. They might not be without cracks, but she knew the glue would hold. Later, after they'd stopped this killer and made sure no more women died, when she was back at Omega and no one was around, then she could fall apart.

While watching him cook, Andrea wondered if Brandon would suggest to Steve that she wasn't Omega material. That he'd seen her in action and she just wouldn't be a good fit long-term.

Maybe it was just time for her to move on altogether.

He brought a plate filled with eggs, bacon and toast and set it in front of her.

"Eat up," he said. "We've got a full day. And night."

She took a bite of her toast and realized how famished she was. He set his own plate down and began eating, also.

Her plate was nearly empty when he asked about last night. She was glad she was nearly done because her food became tasteless. She didn't want to think about last night. Didn't want to face him as she talked about it, knowing what he thought about her. His disgust.

"I wasn't able to pick out anyone in the club who seemed to be acting odd," he said as he took a sip of the coffee. "But then again, I didn't think the killer would actually be there."

"Because you think he follows DJ Shocker in. That he's in the club for the first time that night."

"Maybe not in the club for the first time, but picking his victim then. I was working on a profile last night."

Andrea wasn't sure if he meant while he was at Club Paradise or later while she was sleeping.

"Except for victim two, the truck-stop waitress, all the murders have occurred between twenty-four and forty-eight hours after DJ Shocker's appearance at the club," Brandon continued. "I think the killer picks his victim that night, perhaps the one who is acting the most overtly promiscuous, and comes back to kill her later. But he might come in before, since DJ Shocker's events are so well advertised, to check out potential victims."

"Okay, that's sick, but logical."

"Have you gotten anything over the last couple of nights? Anyone who has seemed out of place?"

She took another sip of her coffee to fortify herself, then looked back down at her plate. She didn't want to eat another bite, but at least it gave her somewhere else to look besides at Brandon.

"It was pretty tough, at first. Filtering through... everything." The barrage of sounds and sights. The unwelcomed touches of men who thought she was cheap. "The first couple of hours of the first night, honestly, I was just trying to survive. Wasn't sure I was going to be able to do it."

"And then what happened?" Brandon's voice was hoarse, almost anguished. She could feel the unhappiness coming from him, but couldn't bring herself to look at his face.

"I don't know. I just had a suck-it-up talk with myself. I had a job to do, and if I didn't, another woman was going to die."

"Sounds like a pretty professional way to think."

For a stripper.

He didn't say it, and she had to admit she didn't even know if he was thinking it. But *she* was.

She still didn't look up from her plate. She took the last bite of her toast that now tasted like cardboard in her mouth.

"Not surprisingly, the overwhelming emotion in the club was lust. Drunken euphoria was a close second. I colored all those in my mind as red and then just ignored them. Guilt—I'm sure more than a few married men were in attendance last night—I colored as green, because I thought that might be worth looking into. Anger and disgust, the key emotions I thought might come from the killer, I tried to color as blue."

"Using colors, that's smart. Did you see any blue?"

"A little." She finally looked at him. "But not from anyone I thought was the killer."

He was too smart not to know she was referring to him. "Andrea—"

She didn't want to talk about his disgust with her. She was holding on by a thin enough thread as it was. She stood up, grabbing their plates.

"You cooked. I'll do dishes. Thanks for breakfast, by the way."

He stood up too and grabbed her wrist gently. "Andrea."

She looked at him, but his face was so intent with something to say she had to look away. She could not do this right now. Not if she had to make it through the entire day and night beyond.

"Brandon, I can't. Not right now. You felt what you

felt. Whatever we have to talk about, can we just do it later?"

"Fine. But I'll do the dishes. You go sit. You'll be on your feet enough today. Plus we have another self-defense lesson in fifteen minutes."

She thought about what had happened with the last self-defense lesson, how they'd ended up in bed all afternoon. "Are you sure that's a good idea?"

"As long as there's a killer around, it's a good idea."

That wasn't what Andrea had meant, but she didn't press it. She just left him to do the dishes and went to sit on the couch. The next thing she knew, Brandon was shaking her awake, gently.

"Come on, lazybones. Nap break is over. Time to do some work." She found his face close to hers, smiling, as she opened her eyes.

She touched his cheek before she remembered she wasn't supposed to. But he didn't pull back as she expected. Instead he leaned forward and kissed her on the forehead.

"I must have fallen asleep for a few minutes," she murmured.

"Try two hours."

Her eyes flew open at that. "Are you serious?"

He smiled again. "It's okay. You needed it. But now it's time to work."

He stood and held his hand down to help her from the couch. She stretched and took it.

"Okay, let's go over our bear-hug move first."

They practiced that a few times and Andrea was pleasantly surprised at what she remembered. What her body automatically remembered. Brandon praised her for it, too.

They spent the next hour going over how to twist out of wrist holds, and the most vulnerable points of an attacker she could hit.

The physical activity, focusing on something besides what was going on between her and Brandon, felt good. She found she had a knack for it, because it was somewhat like dancing, ironically. She just had to think of what step came next. And eventually her body knew what step came next without her having to think about it.

"Okay, one more thing I want to teach today. If someone has you on the ground in a choke hold."

He had Andrea lie on her back and he straddled her hips. He gripped her throat with one hand.

"Most of what I've shown you hasn't been dependent on strength or speed, just on basic human mechanics. Joints only turn certain ways. This is more labor intensive on your part. Someone bigger, heavier, is going to be harder to get off you."

Andrea wasn't sure she could do this. Having Brandon this close in this position? If he slid his hand over they'd be in an embrace rather than in combat. But she tried to focus.

Like all the other techniques he'd shown her, he went over the moves slowly at first: trapping his leg with her foot, grabbing his wrist and elbow, hiking up her hips and flipping him over.

She could do it when he worked with her, but once they started going at a faster speed Andrea had trouble.

"What's the problem?" he asked. "You're going to

have to move more quickly and fluidly than that for it to work."

Andrea gritted her teeth. She didn't think she could do this—he was too big. And she might hurt him. *And* she really did not want to thrust her hips up against his.

"Look, I'm a little tired. Maybe we should just take a break."

Brandon's eyes narrowed as he looked down at her from where he straddled her hips. "Make me."

"I'm serious, Brandon."

The hand that held her throat squeezed a little tighter. Not enough to hurt or cut off her breath. Just enough to make the threat a little real.

She did what he had taught her but her movements were jerky and halfhearted.

"That's not going to be enough. With this move it's not enough to just go through the correct motions. You've got to have some strength behind it. Some fire."

She tried again but the results were the same.

"That's not enough, sweetheart. You've got to do this move like you've got nothing left to lose."

She tried again, chest heaving in frustration when she couldn't budge him.

"Don't call me 'sweetheart,'" she spit out.

"Why?"

"Because you don't think I'm sweet. You think I'm dirty."

"That's right, sweetheart. I'm the jackass who judged you for doing your job the last two nights. I'm the jerk who turned away from you when you needed me to help anchor you. I'm the idiot—"

Andrea let out a cry and did it. Broke his hold, flipped

her body around so she was on top of him. As he hit the ground his air rushed out with a whoosh.

She threw her head back and laughed. "I did it!" She was amazed at the sense of accomplishment.

She felt Brandon's hands resting on her knees. "Yeah, you did. Good job."

She wasn't ready for him to sit up quickly and wrap his arms around her hips, crushing his chest against hers. He buried his face in her neck.

"How I've acted the last two days, what I thought… I was so wrong, sweetheart."

"Brandon—"

"And you're wrong. I don't think you're dirty. I think you're amazing, beautiful, sweet. Seeing you in the club was hard, I'll admit. But it was *my* problem, not yours. You were doing a job. And did it damn well."

She grabbed his face so she could pull him back. He needed to understand. "When I worked before, I wore just as skimpy an outfit. Less, if I was the one onstage. And when I waited tables, I'll admit I flirted to get tips. Encouraged glances and even some touches. I didn't like it but I did it."

He brought his lips reverently to hers. "You did what you had to in order to survive. Being smart enough to work the system to your advantage is not something to be ashamed of. And I promise, I will never make the mistake of judging you for it again."

"But some of what you felt was probably correct."

"Sweetheart, nothing of what I felt was correct. And you've got to stop letting your own head think it was correct, also."

She sighed. "That's easier said than done."

"I spoke to Drackett and he said to give you his personal and professional congratulations for a job well done."

"You spoke to Steve?"

"Last night. And for the record, I agree with him."

"I thought you'd never want to touch me again. That you found me distasteful."

She felt his arms wrap more strongly around her waist before he used his powerful leg muscles to stand up in one fluid motion while still holding her.

"Trust me when I say, I find you more and more tasteful each day I know you." Keeping her legs wrapped around his hips, he carried her back into the bedroom and proceeded to show her.

Chapter Nineteen

If Brandon could've spent all day in bed with Andrea, he would've. He did his best to apologize with both words and actions, trying to say with his body what he wasn't sure she could hear with his words.

He didn't let himself think too much about why it was so important for him to repair what he'd damaged with her. That would lead to too many questions about the future. About how things could never go back to being the same between them at Omega after this case.

The warrior had the woman he craved by his side. That was enough for now.

But they couldn't stay in bed all day, because they still had a killer to catch.

And they were both pretty hungry despite their breakfast.

Andrea was making sandwiches when Brandon came out of the shower. He could tell by the way she moved across the kitchen that she was feeling lighter, happier. The shadows were gone from her eyes.

He should be surprised that she was more attractive with no makeup and messy hair, dancing around in shorts and a loose T-shirt, but he wasn't. Andrea's natural beauty would always outshine what she could do with makeup and a brush.

She felt his presence and turned to smile at him. "Lunch," she said, handing him a plate.

The silence during their meal this time was easy and light. Unlike before. They were washing dishes together when Andrea caught him off guard with her question.

"Hey, do you know who a guy named Damian Freihof is?"

Brandon stilled. She instantly picked up on his nonverbals, stilling and tensing herself.

"What?" she asked.

"Why do you ask who he is?"

"That box my aunt gave me with my stuff. It contained like fifty letters from a Damian Freihof. I have no idea who that is. I think he's got me confused with someone else and has for a long time. I only opened one letter, but they all had the same name and return address on the envelope."

"Can I see them?"

"Do you know him?"

Brandon wouldn't lie to her. He hadn't thought keeping her in the dark about Freihof was a good idea, although he'd agreed because he'd thought there hadn't been any link between Andrea and Freihof since he went away to prison.

But evidently there were fifty links between them.

Steve had been wrong when he thought Freihof had forgotten about Andrea. He sure as hell hadn't forgotten her if he'd written her that many times.

"Yes, I do know who he is. And you do, too. You just don't know that you do."

Andrea's eyes narrowed and he could see her trying to remember. "Was he part of a case I worked? I can't place the name."

"Damian Freihof was one of the three bank robbers/hostage takers you helped stop on the day you met Steve Drackett."

He hated how stress began to fill her body again. "The third guy. The evil one."

"He was the one mostly kept out of the original press reports because of the ties he had with some other bombers and terrorist organizations. We were going to try to use him to catch some bad guys even higher on the food chain, but he decided he'd rather serve a double life sentence."

"Well, evidently he decided to make me his pen pal from prison. That's kind of creepy."

"What did the letter you read say?"

She shrugged. "Nothing threatening. Just that he wished he could've gotten to know me better and looks forward to the time we'll eventually spend together." She shuddered. "That's really frightening now that I know who he is."

"I need to send the letters to Omega, if that's okay. Get someone to check them out."

Andrea shrugged. "Sure. I don't want to read them. Why would Omega want them? Freihof is already serving two life sentences. They're probably not going to find much in the letters that will keep him in jail longer than that."

Brandon put his hands on both her arms. "Freihof

escaped from federal custody last week during a prison transfer. Nobody knows where he is."

ANDREA COULD FEEL all the blood leave her face. "He escaped?"

"Yes." Brandon pulled her in for a hug and she leaned into him for a moment, needing his strength.

Damian Freihof. That was the name of the face that haunted her dreams over the past four years. She had never forgotten his eyes and the evil that had radiated from him in that bank.

She'd asked Steve about him after she'd gone to work for Omega since she'd never heard anything about him in the news. Drackett had assured her that the third man had been arrested, had just been kept out of the press for national-security reasons.

She pulled back from Brandon. "Steve knows Freihof escaped."

"Yes, and we've been keeping our eyes and ears to the ground for info about him. But Steve didn't think Freihof would come after you."

"Why would Steve even think that was a possibility? Before the letters, I wouldn't have thought it was."

Brandon's lips pursed. "During and after his trial, Freihof mentioned coming after you."

"What?"

Brandon shrugged. "Drackett didn't really take it too seriously. Freihof was in custody and he was mad that he was going to jail for the next eighty years. Steve figured the guy was just running his mouth. He also mentioned wanting to kill some other people."

"Why didn't Steve tell me?"

"Freihof was in jail. You were safe."

Andrea took a step back. "But then he got out of jail. Steve should've told me then."

Brandon held out a hand, entreating. "I agree, and even told him so. But this was right as you were coming back here. Steve felt like you had enough on your plate already."

"Well, the last letters are postmarked as late as two weeks ago."

"That's why we need to get them to Omega and see what we can find from them."

"Does anybody know where he is now?"

"He was briefly spotted in Texas. Probably heading to Mexico."

Andrea thought about all the times she'd felt someone watching her over the past few days.

"What about the lightning-storm guy? That could've been Freihof."

Brandon nodded and pulled her back into his arms. "Yes, it could've been. But he would've been taking a huge chance by coming here after you right now. Steve agrees. He's probably heading south."

"So I don't need to worry about him?" That was definitely not going to happen.

"I won't lie to you. Freihof definitely needs to be worried about. Your safety is something Steve and I will be having a heart-to-heart about when we're back at Omega. I'm not going to let anything happen to you, even if it means moving you in with me." She could feel his kisses in her hair. "I just don't think we have to worry about him right at this moment."

Andrea could feel warmth pooling through her. After the brittle cold that had settled on her insides the past couple of days, this felt wonderful. Having someone really care about her felt wonderful. And Brandon had mentioned Omega for the first time, as if what was happening between them would continue.

The thought was both thrilling and terrifying.

She pulled back to look at him, this man who had brought out so many emotions in her over the past week.

"What?" he asked.

"Nothing. Just thinking about life after this case for a second. Realizing that you know just about every single thing there is to know about me, but I don't know much about you."

"You know that I can be a conceited ass who refuses to see the truth that's right in front of him."

She smiled. "Yeah, but I mean the less obvious stuff."

He reached down and bit at her ear in retaliation, then leaned back against the kitchen counter, pulling her with him. "Okay, what do you want to know?"

"How'd you end up at Omega?"

"I was pretty fortunate when I was growing up. My parents realized early that I needed more intellectual challenge than most kids my age or I started acting out physically. That got me on the right path—graduated high school a little early, then found that studying human behavior interested me most."

"So you got a few degrees in it."

He shrugged casually. "Well, schooling came pretty easily to me when I was interested in the subject matter."

"How'd you jump from the academic world to Omega?"

"My best friend since high school, David Vickars. He and I were pretty different in a lot of ways. He was more of an action man. I always tended to think things through and find the most logical solution. He never even went to college. Got all the education he needed from the army, he told me. Anyway, he started working for Omega eight years ago. Pulled me in not long afterward."

Andrea couldn't see his face, the way he was holding her from behind, but could feel the tension, the sadness.

"You guys were partners."

"Yep. A great team, right up until he died a year ago."

"I'm so sorry, Brandon." She turned in his arms so she could face him.

"Me, too. Dave was a good man. Knew when to bend the rules and when to break them. Knew how to keep me in check."

"Do you need to be kept in check a lot?"

Andrea could see the different flecks of emotion cross over his face: sadness, resignation, fear, anger.

"The difference between you and I, sweetheart, is that you have a crooked past but a sweet, pure soul. I'm the opposite—a perfect past with a crooked soul."

Andrea's eyes flew up to his. "What? No, that's not true."

He tucked her hair gently behind both her ears. "Despite all your talents, I'm not sure you can see it because I keep it buried pretty deep. But I think David knew. He always did. That's why he dragged me with him to Omega."

"Knew what?"

"That I've got a darkness in me somewhere. Everything I learned about human behavior and criminal justice in school? I might have used that to be on the opposite side of serial killing if David hadn't gotten me involved with the right side of the law."

Andrea could tell that what Brandon said was true. Or at least he believed it to be so. "You're excellent at your job."

"I'm fascinated by getting inside the head of a killer and figuring out why they do what they do. What mistakes they might make and catching them."

Andrea had no doubt that the beautiful, brilliant man standing with his arms around her could kill someone and get away with it.

He wouldn't make any mistakes.

"With Dave around it was easy to ignore the darkness, to stay out of my own head and stay in the heads of others. Solve crimes. Fight the bad guys. But this last year it's been more difficult." His voice faded to a hushed stillness.

She realized his current demons haunted him as much as her past demons haunted her. He'd kept them a secret from everyone, just as she had.

"I won't let the darkness overtake you," she whispered.

He stiffened, and she was afraid he was going to pull away, maybe even scoff.

Instead, his arms wrapped tightly around her waist and he pulled her to him in a crushing hug, burying his face in her hair. She could feel his breath against her neck, his heart beating against hers.

They held each other for a long while, their embrace keeping all the demons away.

Chapter Twenty

A call came that afternoon from Lance Kendrick at the county sheriff's department. They had found the full phone number from the note Keira had provided.

Jillian Spires had been in contact with Jarrod McConnachie.

Brandon cursed, bringing the receiver down and putting it on speaker so Andrea could hear, too. "Yeah, we talked to him the day after we arrived in town. He was at a local bar, The Boar's Nest, with some of his buddies."

"We were talking to him because he was friends with Noelle Brumby. So that ties him to two of the victims right away," Andrea said.

"He's also attended at least some of DJ Shocker's club tour. We found him in some footage," Kendrick informed them. "So there's another tie-in."

"Damn it," Brandon muttered, rubbing a hand over his face. "To think we'd been so close to him from the very beginning."

"Andrea, is it possible the man you saw in the lightning could've been McConnachie?" Kendrick asked.

She shrugged. "Yes. Jarrod would be the correct build

and weight. It was dark. I was a little freaked out. I didn't get as much detail as I should have."

Brandon slipped an arm around her shoulders. "What's the next step, Kendrick?"

"We've got an APB out on McConnachie. As soon as he's spotted, he'll be arrested. We've also got a warrant to search his place of residence, which ends up is his mother's house. This guy is quite the loser, seems like."

Brandon didn't disagree. "Can we meet your men there?"

"Sure. I'm coming, too." He gave them the address, an isolated area just outside of town.

"We'll see you there in a few."

Brandon disconnected the call.

"Jarrod McConnachie?" Andrea shook her head. "I have to admit, I didn't see that. If it's him, he completely fooled me at the bar on Tuesday."

Brandon nodded. "Me, too. He seemed too sloppy and disorganized. Let's go see what we find at his house."

McConnachie's house, or actually *Mrs. McConnachie's* house, was a small ranch outside of Buckeye. It was in surprisingly good shape based on what they knew about Jarrod, who didn't have a job and spent a lot of his time at bars.

Neither Mrs. McConnachie nor Jarrod were home, but a ranch worker who didn't speak much English and looked very nervous when the police showed up let them into the house.

They searched Jarrod's room first. Brandon and Andrea stood to the side observing as Kendrick and his men methodically looked through the room. It was what you would expect a room of someone who was in his midtwenties, yet didn't have a job and still lived with his mother would look like: unmade bed, collection of high school sports trophies sitting on the shelves, clothes strewn all around.

The officers were methodical and neat in their search. There was no need to destroy any property. They searched under the mattress, in all the drawers and thoroughly in the closet. Brandon was impressed by their thoroughness: he didn't see anywhere they would've missed.

They moved into the living room next, then the kitchen with the same methodical search methods but found nothing of substance. They searched through the mother's room and the other bedroom that had been turned into an office.

Nothing that suggested any crimes or linked Jarrod McConnachie to the women.

The ranch hand who had let them in watched nervously as they moved from room to room. Each room was clean and orderly except for Jarrod's, making the search easier. Brandon stepped outside to look around. They weren't going to find anything in the house, at least nothing concrete.

He could hear Kendrick speaking in Spanish with the nervous worker, explaining something about a work visa. The worker was worried about being deported, not being connected to a crime.

Brandon felt Andrea join him outside the door as he looked at the small barn. "I don't think there's anything in the house. We should check the barn." He called back to Kendrick. "Does the warrant cover the entire property or just the house?"

"All of it," Kendrick broke from his Spanish to respond. They all made their way over to the small structure that was beginning to become run-down.

They almost missed the hatch altogether.

Brandon saw it as they were beginning to turn away after searching the barn: a small hatch leading down into a tiny cellar. It was meant as an emergency hideout during a tornado, and unless you knew it was there, it was easy to miss. It was only big enough to fit two or three people and the hatch door was mostly covered by bags of feed.

He opened the door and turned on the flashlight function of his phone, sliding it down into the dark space. Every law-enforcement officer there, including Brandon, pulled out their weapons as Brandon slowly took the half dozen steps down.

"This is federal agent Brandon Han," he called from the stairs. "I am armed and coming inside. If anyone is in there, make your presence known now."

He waited but no one spoke, so he slowly stepped down. Kendrick stood directly over his shoulder, ready to take a shot. Andrea, since she didn't have a weapon, had done the smart thing and gotten herself out of the way.

Brandon gave himself a few more moments for his eyes to adjust, then rapidly descended the stairs.

No one was in the cellar, but there certainly had been someone there recently.

Pictures of the dead women were all over the boxes that had been placed in the cellar. Pictures of them before they died and right after. There were candles lined all along the walls, as well as a roll of the same white mesh that had been used to cover the women when the police had found them.

This was the killer's preparation room. Might even have been where the killing took place, although getting the bodies up and down those stairs would've been difficult.

Brandon didn't touch anything, just backed out slowly. "Kendrick, call Gerardo Jennison. We need the best crime-scene investigators they've got."

"What is it?" Kendrick asked.

"The killer's preparation room. Jarrod is definitely the guy."

The older man whistled through his teeth before getting on the phone to call for the needed people to work the scene.

Brandon called an officer over to him. "Under no circumstances is anyone to go down there until the CSI people have done their thing. That room is about as pristine as it gets, and we don't want to mess it up."

"Yes, sir," the young officer said.

Brandon looked over at Andrea, shaking his head. "I guess Jarrod fooled both of us."

She nodded. "None of his emotions or nonverbal cues gave him away. I just didn't think he had it in him."

"Me, neither. We didn't give him enough credit."

Kendrick walked over to them. "Crime-scene crew is on their way. And we've got some even better news."

"What's that?" Brandon asked.

"We just picked up Jarrod McConnachie. Idiot went

to The Boar's Nest, just like he goes all the time. Guy had no idea we were onto him. They're holding him in a cell back at the sheriff's office."

"Mind if I question him?" Brandon asked.

Kendrick slapped him on the back. "I was hoping you would."

As MUCH AS Andrea was saddened by the thought of Jarrod—someone she had known in high school and who had seemed friendly—as the killer, she was thankful that his arrest meant she didn't have to go work at Club Paradise that night.

Missing the DJ Shocker circus wasn't upsetting at all. Andrea was ready to retire her bustier and short skirts forever. Those days were well and truly in her past.

She wished she could talk Keira into doing the same, but knew no one talked Keira into anything. She would do it when she was ready.

Andrea was on her way to see her friend now. Brandon had ridden with the local police back to the sheriff's office to question Jarrod. Andrea would meet him there soon. But she wanted to talk to Keira first. Let Keira know that things were better between her and Brandon. She would show her Jarrod's picture while she was there, see if that jogged her memory any.

Hopefully Brandon could get a confession out of Jarrod. That would tie up the most loose ends. And then they'd be heading back to Omega.

Honestly, Andrea wasn't sure what that would mean for the two of them. But she knew, either way, it was time for her to make some changes in her life. Keeping herself distant from everyone at Omega wasn't the way she wanted to live any longer.

She pulled up to Keira's apartment, a small one not far from where Andrea had lived during her time in Buckeye, and knocked on the door. Keira hugged her as she pulled her inside.

"Hey, sweetie, what's going on?" Her hair was up in giant rollers and she had the TV remote in her hand. "I'm just catching up on my television viewing."

Andrea looked, expecting to see some drama or sitcom, but found some sort of wildlife documentary on the TV. Interesting choice.

"Just came to ask if you'd ever seen this guy hanging around Jillian. We think he might be the killer."

Keira took the picture. "Yes. Absolutely yes. More than once. But I don't know his name or how to get ahold of him or anything."

"That's okay. He's already been arrested. His name is Jarrod McConnachie. He and I actually went to high school together before I dropped out."

"Jarrod McConnachie. Bastard." She studied the picture a minute more before handing it back to Andrea. "I'm glad you guys got him."

"Yeah, me too." Andrea looked over at the TV again as Keira put it on Pause. "And I also wanted to let you know that things are much better with Brandon and me."

Keira reached up and patted Andrea on the cheek. "I'm glad. And I'm not surprised. That man is crazy about you, girl."

Andrea laughed ruefully. "I'm not so sure about that.

But we're at least doing better. He apologized for getting upset about me at Club Paradise."

"I'd like to hear more about how exactly he apologized—" Keira waggled her eyebrows "—but I'm sure you wouldn't give me the juicy deets anyway."

Andrea felt her face heat.

Keira laughed. "I thought so. He seems like a good man, Andrea."

"He is."

"And more than that, you're a good woman. Past is past. Future is future."

Andrea nodded and grabbed the shorter woman in for a hug. "I'm learning that. In no small part, thanks to you."

"Good. You're a beautiful, compassionate, intelligent, classy lady. Don't you ever forget that."

Andrea could feel tears brimming in her eyes. "Thank you, Keira."

"All right, enough with all the girl talk. You're welcome to stay here and watch my shows with me until I head into work."

"No, I'm going to the station. Help Brandon question the suspect if I can."

"Then I'll catch you later." Keira winked. "Hopefully not as long as it's been since the last time I saw you."

"I promise."

Andrea said her goodbyes and made her way out to her car. There was no message from Brandon, so evidently nothing new with Jarrod.

Andrea pulled the car out of the apartment complex and began driving north up Highway 85 toward the sheriff's office. She passed Jaguar's, slowing as she did so.

She wasn't going to let that place have a hold over her life anymore. As Keira had said, past was past. Future was future. Jaguar's belonged in her past. She sped up, leaving it behind her.

She saw a car pulled over on the side of the road a few miles outside of town in the direction of the sheriff's office, smoke billowing from the hood. Andrea slowed, not wanting to put herself in a dangerous situation, but not wanting to leave someone stranded in the desert as it began to get dark.

A plump older lady was leaning over her engine, wringing her hands. No one else seemed to be nearby.

Andrea pulled her car over. The least she could do was offer a ride or to call someone.

"Ma'am? Are you okay?"

The woman—a little heavy and probably in her late fifties—looked over at Andrea gratefully. "Oh, honey, thank you so much for stopping! I was afraid no one was going to come along this road. Something is happening with my engine."

Andrea came to stand over next to the woman. "I don't really know anything about cars. But I'd be glad to call someone for you or give you a ride."

The woman looked vaguely familiar to Andrea, probably someone she had known when she lived here, or maybe even one of Aunt Margaret's friends. But honestly, Andrea didn't want to know. Didn't want to answer questions if the woman did know her from when she was younger.

The woman's primary emotion seemed to be anger, and maybe some firm resolution, but neither of those were unusual, given the circumstances. She could be angry at her husband for not servicing the car properly, or maybe just angry that she'd broken down in the middle of nowhere.

"That's so nice of you, dear." The woman began to walk around to the back of her car. "Can you just come back here and help me carry these cables to the front? I think I might be able to do what my husband did to it last time this happened."

Andrea followed her, but really didn't want to stick around while the woman tried to fix her car. Andrea would help carry whatever cables, then would offer again to give her a ride or call someone. She couldn't spend hours on the side of the road.

She wanted to get back to Brandon.

She walked back and opened up the trunk for the woman. It was completely empty.

"Um, ma'am, there are no cables back he—" Andrea felt a sharp sting in her neck. She reached up to swat away whatever insect had gotten her.

Almost immediately she began to feel dizzy as the world swam around her.

"What?" She tried to focus on the woman, who pushed Andrea down into the trunk.

"Shame on you." The bitterness in the woman's eyes was clear now, although Andrea couldn't seem to focus on them. "You're just as bad as those other hussies. Leading men astray. You're even worse, since you pretend to be the police, too. But I will make sure you're purified."

The last thing Andrea processed was the trunk closing over her before the darkness pulled her under.

Chapter Twenty-One

Even before going in to question Jarrod, Brandon tried to verify the man's whereabouts during the murders. Jarrod had been at all the strip clubs for the DJ Shocker tour where the dead dancers worked. And sure enough, he *hadn't* been at the tour stop for the night the truck-stop waitress was killed.

Probably because he was too busy killing her.

Jarrod's friends, not knowing Jarrod was in custody or suspected of multiple murders, had given Brandon all the information they had. They'd been glad to talk about the DJ Shocker tour; it had been a hoot for them. They'd all independently backed up each other's stories, with just enough details—but not the same details—for Brandon to highly suspect they were being authentic in their responses.

He wished he had Andrea here to get her opinion on whether the men were telling the truth, but she'd gone to talk to Keira. She'd be here soon and he could at least get her opinion on Jarrod's nonverbal behavior.

Because, despite Jarrod's friends' confirmation of his location at the clubs and even despite what they had found in the cellar at his house, Brandon still had doubts that Jarrod was the killer.

He watched Jarrod through the two-way mirror where he sat in the interrogation room. Everything about the man was unkempt. He had on a wrinkled shirt and dirty jeans. His greasy hair needed washing and he looked as if he'd forgotten to shave for the past four days at least. Not to mention the man had been picked up at the bar he frequented. He hadn't even tried to avoid law enforcement.

Brandon found it difficult to reconcile these aspects of the man's personality with the cold, calculating nature of the purity killer. But maybe it was a disguise. Maybe Jarrod had fooled both him and Andrea, and Brandon's pride just didn't want him to admit it.

God knew he'd been wrong an awful lot this week.

Brandon knew where he would start the questioning: victim number two, Ashley Judson, the waitress who dabbled with prostitution on the side. She was the one who didn't fit in the Angels and Devils tour theory. She didn't dance, wasn't a stripper. If Jarrod had picked all his other victims at strip clubs, what had led him to pick her, also?

Brandon glanced at his watch. Andrea should be here any minute. He would go ahead and get started.

"Hi, Jarrod. Remember me?" Brandon walked in the door and took the seat across from Jarrod.

Jarrod nodded slowly. "Yeah. You're that cop that was with Andrea at The Boar's Nest last week. Why am I here, man? I told you everything I knew about Noelle then."

Brandon wanted answers, but more than that he

wanted to make sure Jarrod went to jail for the crimes he'd committed. He certainly didn't want him to get off on any technicalities. He would make sure his questioning fell well within the letter of the law. Having a law degree helped make that easier.

Brandon read Jarrod his Miranda rights.

"Yeah, yeah. They already read me my rights when they picked me up at the bar."

"I just want to make sure you know them. That you can call a lawyer if you want to."

Brandon hoped he didn't want to. A lawyer would stall every question he had for Jarrod. He prayed Jarrod would think he was too smart to need a lawyer.

"Naw, I don't need one." Jarrod sat back in his chair. "I don't got anything to hide."

Brandon smiled. If Jarrod was a wiser man he would've been wary.

Jarrod wasn't.

Brandon took out a picture of Ashley Judson, victim number two—a candid shot, a copy of one Brandon had seen hanging in the cellar at Jarrod's house. He slid it over so Jarrod could see it.

"Do you know this girl?"

"Um… I'm not sure."

There was no doubt in Brandon's mind that Jarrod recognized her. Even if they hadn't just found that picture *at Jarrod's house*, his nonverbal behavior—looking over to the side and down—was giving him away.

"I think you do know her, Jarrod."

Jarrod shrugged. "Maybe. I know a lot of girls."

"How about these? Do you know any of them?"

Brandon took out pictures of the women—all copies

of the ones they had found on Jarrod's property—and placed them on the table one after another.

Jarrod's face seemed to lose more color with each picture he studied.

"What's going on here?" he finally asked.

"Why don't you tell me?" Brandon sat back and crossed his arms over his chest.

"What exactly do you want to know? I know Noelle is dead. And I know I told you I didn't really know her very well, but fine, I slept with her, okay? It was a fling. She was getting off of work and I was bored. But I didn't kill her."

"And what about her?" He pointed to the waitress.

"What? Okay, fine. I slept with her, too." He spread his arms out wide across the pictures. "Great, yes. I slept with all these women. Is that a crime? It's pretty damn freaky that the cops are taking a picture of all the girls I've banged over the last month."

Brandon's eyes narrowed. Either Jarrod was the best actor he'd ever seen, or he didn't have any idea all these women were dead.

"How'd you like these girls, Jarrod? Going to see any of them again? Not Noelle of course, but the others?"

Jarrod shrugged one shoulder. "I don't know. Maybe Jillian. She's pretty hot. A dancer." He pointed at Jillian's picture, the woman who had worked at Jaguar's.

"All of them are dancers, right?"

"Not this one." He gestured to Ashley Judson. "She's a waitress."

Brandon smiled, tilting his head to the side. He doubted Jarrod would notice his smile didn't come anywhere near his eyes. "Yeah, I heard that's not all she does. I heard she has a little business on the side with truckers or whoever's willing to pay." Brandon winked.

"Is that what this is about? You think I paid for sex? I didn't pay Ashley, man. It was completely mutual between the two of us. You can ask her."

It was time to move in for the kill. To see if he could force Jarrod into admitting something. All he needed to do was slip up that he knew any of the girls besides Noelle was dead and Brandon would have him trapped in a lie. Then it would just be a matter of wearing him down.

"No, I don't care about money. But doesn't it bother you that Ashley was a hooker on the side? All these girls you've been with aren't exactly upstanding members of society."

Jarrod grimaced. "I don't care about that sort of stuff, man. The girls were fun. I like fun girls."

"You sure about that, Jarrod? Sure you didn't realize that these girls needed cleaning up? That they were tramps? That this town would be better off without them?"

"What?" Jarrod's face wrinkled.

"You know, maybe they needed to be purified in some way. Help them get on the right track? Find God or peace or whatever?"

Jarrod let out a breath, shaking his head. "Dude. You are starting to sound just like my mom. I'm not into that sort of purity stuff. I like girls who like to have a good time. I'm not looking for someone to settle down with. I keep trying to explain that to her."

Brandon sat up a little straighter in his chair. "Your mom talks about purity a lot?"

"All. The. Time." Jarrod rolled his eyes. "I think I'm going to have to move out of her house. The lectures I get after staying out late… Unbelievable. And if she knew I was going to strip clubs? *Sleeping* with girls from strip clubs? She'd blow a gasket. Not enough prayers that could be said for my soul."

Brandon stood up. They had the wrong man. In fact, there wasn't a *man* at all. Jarrod's mother was the serial killer.

He walked over and buzzed the door to let him out. Surely Andrea was here by now. Brandon realized that having her to talk things through with had become important to him over the past few days. After David, he never thought he'd have that again. Never thought he'd want to.

Andrea wasn't in the observation room, but Kendrick was.

"You get that?" Brandon asked him.

"We're already putting an APB out on her. She's not at their house. We've still got people there."

"Have you seen Andrea?"

"No. She hasn't been here at all."

Something clenched in Brandon's stomach. He reached for his phone and dialed her number, knowing texts weren't great for her. It rang then went to voice mail. He left a message, then called Keira next.

"Glad to hear you aren't a complete ass after all," Keira said by way of greeting.

Any other time he would've joked with Keira, even apologized and thanked her. But not now. "Andrea with you, Keira?"

"No, left about forty-five minutes ago. Said you had

the killer in custody. Showed me a picture of him. I recognized him as someone Jillian hung out with."

"He's not the right person. Stay in your house until you hear from me. Get a call out to all the girls at Jaguar's if you can. The killer is still out there."

Keira was silent for just a moment. "Okay. Find our girl, Brandon. And have her call me when you do."

"I will."

Brandon put a call in to Big Mike at Club Paradise to make sure Andrea hadn't gone there to tell him the good news. Mike hadn't seen her.

Brandon tried her phone again. Nothing.

Kendrick reentered the observation room. His face was grim.

"Your rental a white Toyota?" He read off a license-plate number.

Brandon nodded.

"It was found abandoned off Highway 85. The phone you're trying to call was inside."

Chapter Twenty-Two

Andrea fought to claw her way out of the darkness. Her brain didn't want to focus; her eyes didn't want to open. Reality felt distant, fuzzy. Her hands were tied behind her back and she was lying on her side; that much she knew.

She forced herself to be still, to think, to try to figure out what was going on.

She'd been drugged by that lady she'd stopped to help on the side of the road. She forced back nausea as she thought of the woman's face, how it had seemed vaguely familiar.

"I know you're waking up," Andrea heard the woman say from a few yards away. "I didn't give you enough tranquilizer for you to be out for too long."

Andrea remembered being pushed into a trunk, but they weren't in a car any longer. She opened her eyes in the smallest of slits, trying to keep the nausea at bay. They weren't outside. Somewhere inside, but mostly empty. Maybe a small abandoned warehouse? She opened her eyes a little more and saw where the older woman was sitting.

On a pew. An abandoned church building. It looked as if most of it had been burned in a fire.

Given the nature of the crimes, it made perfect sense that this was where the killer would bring the victims.

"I know your aunt, you know," the woman said from where she sat. "Met her at an AA meeting. Not that I'm an alcoholic, but my son is. I thought learning about AA might help me help him. He needs help. Needs to be shown the right path. He's so weak."

It came to Andrea then. They'd had the right house, but the wrong killer.

"You're Jarrod's mother."

"Yes."

Andrea tried to shake off the mental cobwebs clouding her mind. To think. To find some way to relate to this woman. "He and I went to high school together."

"Before you dropped out. Margaret told me."

"Jarrod is my friend. I know he wouldn't want you to hurt me."

"Jarrod doesn't know what he wants. And all you women keep trying to corrupt him. Lead him astray. It's been my job as a mother to clean up after him. To remove temptation from his sight."

"So you killed the women Jarrod was interested in."

"I removed the harlots who led him astray. All of them tempted him beyond what he could bear. All of them either removed their clothes or had sex for money." Mrs. McConnachie stood up. "All I did was what any other mother would do."

"But you killed them."

She took a step closer. "No. I stopped them from

committing any further sins. From tempting any other men like Jarrod and corrupting them."

There was no reasoning with this woman about what she had done. Andrea could feel the sincerity radiating from her. In Mrs. McConnachie's mind, her actions were both logical and just. Andrea needed to use another tactic.

"I didn't corrupt Jarrod. He and I have never been romantically involved."

That stopped Mrs. McConnachie for just a moment. She frowned and looked down at her hands. Andrea realized she was holding a rope. No doubt the same one she'd used to strangle the other women.

Andrea began to slide backward on the floor, away from her.

That was a mistake.

Her eyes narrowed and she stepped toward Andrea.

"No. You work at one of those disgusting clubs. I saw you."

"Mrs. McConnachie, I was working undercover." *Trying to catch you*, but Andrea knew not to say that. "I was trying to stop the same thing you were trying to stop, women from corrupting men."

Mrs. McConnachie stopped again, but then shook her head. "No. Margaret said you two had talked, but you wouldn't forgive her, that you were still angry at her even though she had taken you in to raise when you were younger. You're just as bad as those women who tried to corrupt Jarrod."

Andrea realized the older woman wasn't interested in reason or logic. She planned to kill Andrea. The action was already justified in her mind.

Where was Brandon? Had he realized yet Jarrod wasn't the killer? Andrea had no doubt he would; she just didn't think it would be in time to save her. She had no idea where she was. How could Brandon possibly know?

Andrea scooted away on the floor as Jarrod's mother walked toward her. She tried to think of any of the self-defense techniques Brandon had taught her, but with her arms restrained and body feeling so sluggish because of the drugs, it was difficult to move, much less fight.

Tears filled Andrea's eyes. She was going to die here. Killed, ironically, by the very embodiment of a demon from her past, just as Andrea was starting to truly put the past behind her.

She'd never know what could've been between her and Brandon.

Mrs. McConnachie pulled her up into a kneeling position and quickly wrapped her strand of rope around Andrea's neck, coming to stand behind her. Andrea struggled not to fall over, knowing that would just quicken the strangulation.

"Don't worry. This won't hurt very long. Soon you'll be at peace."

Andrea felt the bite of the rope against her throat, instantly cutting off her air. She couldn't help but struggle although it didn't do any good. Her arms bit against the restraints, she could feel blood, but couldn't get loose.

She tried to suck in a breath but the sound just came out as a hoarse sigh.

"There, there," Mrs. McConnachie crooned. "Don't

fight it. Find your peace. That's all you need to do now."

Andrea fought one last time, trying to throw her weight to the side, to not panic as Brandon had taught her to do. But it was no use.

Blessed blackness was overtaking Andrea when the pressure suddenly lessened. She collapsed to her side as Mrs. McConnachie fell to the ground next to her. Andrea sucked life-giving oxygen as she tried to figure out what had happened. Had Brandon found them?

Jarrod's mother's eyes stared blankly ahead as a pool of blood began to surround her on the ground. The woman was dead. Andrea couldn't get her body to the angle she needed to prop herself up. All she could do was barely hold on to consciousness as she struggled to get air through her bruised throat.

"Have you ever heard anything so tedious in your entire life as that woman carrying on?" A foot kicked Mrs. McConnachie's body to the side, then squatted down next to Andrea so she could see his face.

She immediately recognized the evil-laden eyes of Damian Freihof.

This time she didn't even try to fight the blackness as it pulled her under.

THE WARRIOR INSIDE Brandon roared to life. Andrea—*his woman*—was in danger, the most desperate kind of danger. Brandon had to do something about that.

He was turning to go back and demand answers from Jarrod—he didn't plan to be anywhere near so gentle this time—when Kendrick put his hand on Brandon's arm to stop him. He took a slight step back when Brandon turned his ferocious gaze on him.

"What?" Brandon snapped out. Kendrick, whatever good he meant, was standing in his way from getting to Andrea.

No one, not even law enforcement, was going to stop him from finding her. By whatever means necessary.

"Whoa, Han." The man held up both hands in a gesture of surrender. "Before you go in there, I just wanted you to know that a vehicle in distress was called in by a civilian near where Andrea's car was found about thirty minutes ago."

Brandon listened. This could be useful intel. "Okay."

"Lady didn't want to stop because she had two babies in the car, but didn't want to leave what looked to be like an older woman stranded. She doesn't remember the exact model of the vehicle, but it was a black four-door sedan. 'Like something from the '80s,' the woman said."

"I'm going to question Jarrod," Brandon told him. "This may not be pretty. I'd appreciate it if there were no interruptions."

Kendrick shrugged. "Actually, I'm going back out to the McConnachies' ranch, make sure there's no unknown buildings where the mom might have Andrea. I'm going to send our other men out to look around town. I'll call Phoenix police department and see if we can get some help, too."

"Good. Keep me posted."

Kendrick handed Brandon the keys to a squad car, then shrugged, turning away. "And damn if the system that records our interrogation-room interviews isn't on the fritz again."

Brandon nodded curtly. He would thank Kendrick later. After he had Andrea back safely.

He unlocked the interview-room door from the outside so he would be able to get back out, then slipped inside. Jarrod was still sitting there, looking bored, biting unkempt fingernails.

"Does your mother drive a black sedan? Late '80s-ish model?"

Jarrod rolled his eyes. "Oh my gosh, yes. She's had that thing since before I was born. I'm embarrassed whenever I have to borrow it."

Brandon refrained from mentioning that Jarrod was in his midtwenties and should have his own damn car.

"Where does your mother like to hang out, Jarrod?"

"Why?" Jarrod snickered. "You looking for a date? I'm sure she wouldn't be much fun, you know."

Brandon rammed his fist down on the table. Jarrod flew back in his chair, eyes wide.

"What the hell, man?"

"I'll tell you what the hell." Brandon reached down and got the autopsy photographs of each of the dead women. He put them on top of the photographs of when they were alive. "Do you know why you're here, Jarrod? Because every single one of the women you had a fling with over the last few weeks is dead."

Jarrod looked as if he was going to vomit. Color leaked from his face. "I didn't do this, man. I swear to God, I didn't kill them. I have an alibi, remember?"

Under other circumstances Brandon would have handled a situation like this more delicately, broken the news to him more gently. Jarrod's mom might be a killer, but the woman was still his mother.

Brandon didn't have that kind of time.

"I know you didn't kill them. Your mother did."

Brandon's eyes bugged right out of his head. "What?"

"She must have been following you. She saw the women you hooked up with and killed them the next day or soon after."

"But...but why?"

"You said she talks about purification all the time? These women's bodies were left with purification rituals. Like your mother was cleansing them to send them to the next world or whatever."

The final bit of color left Jarrod's complexion. "She talks about that sort of junk all the time." He blanched as he tore his eyes up from the pictures to look at Brandon where he leaned on both arms against the table. "About needing to clean up the 'riffraff' in this town, to get rid of all those who would lead men down a corrupted path. I think my dad might have cheated on her or something before he died. But I never knew she meant to kill anyone. I just thought she meant starting a petition to close down the local strip clubs or something, you know?"

"Jarrod, I know this is hard. But I need your help *right now*. Another woman's life is at stake. Andrea's."

Jarrod was staring down at the pictures again.

"Where would your mom do this, Jarrod? Kill these women. We've already checked your house and barn. Is there anywhere else on your property?"

Jarrod shook his head numbly. "We don't really own anything besides the house and barn. Most of the land got sold off when Dad died."

"Okay, then somewhere else? Where does your mom like to go? Where does she hang out?"

Jarrod said nothing, just stared at the pictures. Brandon knew he was losing the other man, shock settling in. That was unacceptable until he got the info he needed.

He reached down and grabbed Jarrod by the collar of the cheap jacket he wore and yanked him out of his chair. Under any other circumstances this sort of man-handling of a witness would be completely unacceptable. This wasn't some action movie where cops could do whatever they wanted with no repercussions.

Brandon didn't give a damn about repercussions.

"Think, Jarrod. Where would your mother go to do these things?" He shook the other man.

"I don't know. She goes to church a lot and some other meetings. I don't really know what." His voice was squeaky.

"No. It couldn't be a place other people are around. Where else? Where would she go if she wanted to be alone?"

Jarrod began to cry. Brandon pulled the younger man's face closer to his.

"Focus, Jarrod. Your mother would need to be somewhere where no one is around. Isolated, to at least some degree. Where. Would. She. Go?" He punctuated each word with a shake.

"I don't know, man, maybe the old church off Highway 85? She always slows down when we drive past. It's where my dad's memorial service was held."

"No, a church is too crowded, even if no service is going on."

Jarrod shook his head. "No, this one burned a few

years ago. Congregation decided to build a new church in a more convenient location rather than pay to have that one rebuilt. The outer walls are still standing but the inside is pretty torn up."

That was it. It had to be.

"Where, exactly?"

Jarrod quickly explained, and Brandon was flying out the door and to the squad car in seconds, praying he wasn't too late.

Chapter Twenty-Three

Brandon parked the squad car and got out of it silently, not wanting to take the chance that Mrs. McConnachie might hear him and panic, hurting Andrea.

But he sprinted because the woman had already had Andrea in her clutches for way too long. Brandon pushed the warrior, who wanted to burst in and *fight*, aside. Logic had to reign right now. Caution. The mental state of Mrs. McConnachie was unknown. He'd radioed for help, but wasn't going to wait for backup to arrive.

Brandon eased his way through a side door that couldn't be completely closed because of burn damage. He couldn't see most of the larger section of the charred church, only the front portion near what must have once been the altar area. Brandon was shocked at what met his eyes.

Mrs. McConnachie's dead body lying on the ground.

Brandon no longer worried about silence or caution. Had Andrea been wounded in fighting the older woman? Did she need medical attention? He was glad it was Mrs. McConnachie on the ground and not Andrea, but where was she?

He burst into the room, looking around, but didn't see her. Had she made her way outside? He began looking between pews, to make sure she hadn't fallen behind one.

He sensed her behind him before he saw or heard her. Brandon turned to find Andrea standing in the aisle between the two rows of pews, as if she was a bride about to walk to her groom.

But in the shadows behind Andrea, Brandon could immediately make out another presence. He knew right away who it was.

"Let her go, Freihof."

"Ah, Agent Han, I see my reputation has preceded me."

"Yeah, your reputation as a sicko. Let her go."

"Come now, Agent Han, I'm sure *sicko* isn't the clinical term. You have too many degrees to be using such common terminology."

Brandon's eyes narrowed, but he played along. "How about 'psychopath with homicidal tendencies and sociopathic and delusional proclivity.'"

"Yes, yes. So much better!" Freihof turned to Andrea, shrugging. "Basically a sicko."

Freihof took a few steps closer, forcing Andrea with him as a shield, coming out of the shadows and into the dim light of the church. Brandon could see the knife Freihof held at her throat, which was covered with angry red marks. Andrea had been strangled.

"Miss Gordon unfortunately fell into the clutches of the crazy old lady there." Freihof gestured toward Mrs. McConnachie's body. "I had to take care of that. Wasn't going to let anyone kill our Andrea."

He kissed Andrea's cheek and she flinched. "Anyone but me, that is. Please take your gun out and throw it to the side, Agent Han."

Andrea tried to move away, but Freihof pulled her back against him, his blade still at her throat. Brandon took his Glock out of its holster and slid it on the ground over to the side. He refused to take a chance on Freihof cutting Andrea's throat. Freihof nodded approvingly.

"I've had almost four years to study you all," Freihof continued. "It's amazing how much one can find out about Omega Sector if he tries, both by electronic and flesh-and-blood sources. Not to mention, your organization has put a lot of people behind bars. A lot of *angry* people."

"What do you want, Freihof?" Brandon asked. He needed to get Andrea away from Freihof's blade.

"C'mon, Agent Han, play along. I'm just trying to impress you with my knowledge. I know Steve Drackett is your boss and was there the night I was arrested. I know a great deal about some of your colleagues, a Liam Goetz and Joe Matarazzo. More than that."

Brandon tried to figure out the other man's endgame, in order to get ahead of him, but couldn't see it. "Great, Freihof. I am thoroughly impressed at your mental database of Omega Sector."

Freihof smiled and shook his head back and forth like a giddy child, taking a few steps closer with Andrea. "I know. I'm showing off. It's annoying, I'm sure."

He had figured the man was a psychopath, but Brandon hadn't realized just how intelligent he was.

Freihof's size and strength were also impressive. He'd obviously spent some of his time in prison working out and bulking up.

Freihof was dangerous in every possible way.

"Okay." Brandon took a step closer, arms outstretched. "Honestly, I am pretty impressed. Your escape. Finding us. Knowing so much about Omega. You're definitely more advanced than most of the criminals I face."

"Thank you, Dr. Han. It means a lot that you would say that."

"Now tell me what you want, and let Andrea go."

Brandon purposefully did not let himself look at her. He didn't want to give away how much she meant to him, plus couldn't trust himself to be able to focus if he saw she was about to fall apart.

Andrea was strong. She could handle it. He had to believe that. He did believe it.

Freihof's knife stayed at her neck. "What I want? Do you mean long-term or short-term?"

"Either."

"What I want, what I plan to do long-term, is take Omega Sector apart piece by piece. Destroy you guys from within until the whole organization falls apart. And keep Andrea here by my side as a plaything while I do it."

Over Brandon's dead body. "Some grandiose plans you got there. How about short-term?"

"Short-term, I plan to sit Miss Gordon down right here at this pew—oh, please don't get me started about the church symbolism—and give her a little gift."

Freihof did as he'd spoken and sat Andrea down, awkwardly because her hands were restrained behind her back, on the pew next to him. Brandon watched in horror as he took out a small explosive device with a twine loop and wrapped it like a necklace around Andrea's slender neck. He took her hands and secured them to the arm of one of the pews with a zip tie.

Brandon could see the three-minute countdown blinking out at him brightly.

"I know we're running out of time and the rest of this rinky-dink town's police force will be here soon, so I'm going to start this timer," Freihof continued in a conversational tone. "That will give you three minutes to finish me off and get back to your love here, Dr. Han."

"Don't turn that thing on," Brandon said through clenched teeth. "How's she supposed to be your long-term plaything if you blow her up?"

"I've found you have to be flexible in your plans, Agent Han. Besides, I don't foresee any problem with me being able to take you in three minutes—it will give us both motivation to do our best work, right? Neither of us wants Andrea in little pieces."

Freihof pressed a button that started the countdown. 2:59, 2:58, 2:57...

"I have a feeling you're going to wish you'd spent less time in the library and more time in the gym, Dr. Han." Freihof's eyes were complete evil.

Brandon allowed himself to look at Andrea just for a moment. A single tear fell from her green eyes. Then he looked down at the explosives attached to her neck. 2:51, 2:50...

Freihof was wrong. Brandon wasn't going to wish he'd spent more time at the gym. He stood up straighter, immediately knowing what he had to do. For the first time in his entire life, Brandon didn't even try to keep the darkness inside him at bay. He let the cold, intellectual side of himself be pushed to the side.

As the warrior inside broke free.

He could feel his mind emptying, a complete and utter focus overtaking him. Intellect would not win this battle; the warrior would.

The warrior fighting for his woman.

He saw Freihof's eyes narrow briefly—the man realized his mistake too late—before Brandon flew at him at a speed he wasn't expecting. Freihof still had the knife, and Brandon felt its sharp sting, but it seemed to be at a distance.

Freihof was bigger, stronger and had a weapon. But Brandon fought like a man with nothing to lose.

Because he realized what the warrior inside him had known all along: if he lost Andrea, he lost everything.

The blows between him and Freihof were brutal and coarse. The countdown around Andrea's neck left no room for strategy, no room to dance around each other.

Brandon felt perverse pleasure as Freihof's nose broke under one of his punches, but then felt the burn as the man's knife found his side. Again.

The moves he'd practiced so recently with Andrea helped him face the bigger man. He heard the snap of Freihof's arm and the man's grunt of pain when Brandon used a move he had just been showing her yesterday.

The only thing the warrior would allow his intellectual side to do was keep track of the time. Without even having to look, Brandon knew the exact second of the counter.

1:02, 1:01, 1:00...

As Freihof fell to the ground, Brandon threw punch

after punch at the man's head and torso. Brandon knew at that point he would win the fight.

But he also knew he would pay a heavy price. He could feel himself becoming light-headed from blood loss, although he'd since kicked Freihof's knife away.

0:19, 0:18, 0:17…

He had Freihof in the hold he wanted. One that would subdue him into unconsciousness in a matter of seconds.

"You're running out of time, Han." Freihof wheezed. "Are you going to choose her or me?"

He was right. Brandon didn't even hesitate. He let Freihof go and ran over to Andrea.

0:10…

He had no idea how to disarm the bomb; all he could do was get it off her and away from them, praying it would not have enough power to bring the entire building down on them.

0:06, 0:05…

He slipped it off her neck and threw it as far as he could toward the back corner of the church. He snatched the knife lying beside Freihof's unconscious form and cut through the zip tie and most of the thin twine that bound Andrea's wrists. That was all he could do.

He grabbed her and slid them both under a pew, wrapping himself around her to protect her as best he could, tucking her head into his chest.

A moment later the explosion shook the entire building and nothing could be seen but darkness.

EVERYTHING IN ANDREA'S body hurt. Her shoulders, her throat, her ears. But she was still alive.

The building hadn't collapsed, but given the state it had already been in before the explosion, Andrea wasn't sure how long it would stay standing.

"Brandon, are you okay? I think we need to get out of here."

She nudged him with her shoulder. He had pulled her close to protect her, but now his arms were lying limply by his side. The bonds that held her wrists were looser and Andrea tugged at them for release. Seeing Brandon lying so still gave her a burst of strength.

She bit her lip in agony as her shoulders moved back into a more natural position.

"Brandon?" More panicked now, she brought her cheek up to his mouth to see if she could feel his breath. Yes, breathing. But when she looked down at his body all she saw was blood.

Too much blood.

She tried to stop the bleeding with her hands, but his shirt was so soaked she couldn't even figure out where the wounds were.

"This is the Maricopa County Sheriff's Department," Andrea heard someone call out. "Is anyone in here?"

"Yes," she yelled as loud as her hoarse voice would allow. "Back here."

She waved her hand, but then immediately brought it back down to his wounds.

Too much blood.

"Here," she called out again. Flashlights pointed in her direction as she called out. "I need help." Her voice completely gave out with that last word.

Out of the corner of her eye, something caught her

attention. Freihof. She turned and he gave her a tiny wave and evil smile before running silently out the side door.

Andrea wanted to communicate with the police officers who were making their way through the rubble to get to them. To tell them about Freihof, but she literally could not get the words out.

Besides, she didn't care about Freihof when Brandon's blood was seeping out of his body under her. He still wasn't conscious.

She bent back down to say in his ear as loudly as her voice would allow, "Come on, Brandon. I need you. I've had two serial killers almost get me today and we're not going to let them win. You fought for me. You beat him for me. Fight for *you* now. *For us.*"

She kissed him. His lips, his forehead, his cheeks.

A paramedic as well as two police officers came and took over life-saving duties. Andrea didn't want to let Brandon go but knew more qualified people needed to take over. She watched it all as if she was in a daze.

But when they rushed Brandon into the ambulance, Andrea found her spirit and fought to stay with him. She wasn't letting Brandon out of her sight. A paramedic stopped her at the ambulance door.

"I'm sorry—you can't ride here."

"I have to," Andrea croaked out, but the words came out soundless. She could feel herself begin to panic. She couldn't leave Brandon alone.

She felt someone take her arm. "I'll drive you," Kendrick said. "Consider it the beginning of restitution for all the times we let you down when you were younger."

Andrea nodded. She knew she should say something, couldn't anyway, so she just got in the car with Kendrick. Her eyes never left the ambulance the entire time.

Chapter Twenty-Four

Fifteen hours later—the longest fifteen hours of her life—Brandon was safely out of surgery. Andrea was still watching over him. Keira had brought her a change of clothes, much needed since hers had been covered in Brandon's blood. Andrea had talked with her friend for a while, still a difficult task due to the damage to her throat. Keira had contacted Steve Drackett for Andrea so he could be updated.

The doctors had done a full scan of Andrea after Kendrick brought her in right behind Brandon. She'd been very fortunate, they'd told her, that although she had extensive bruising and swelling, none of her neck muscles had been ruptured, nor did there seem to be any permanent damage to her larynx.

Ironically, if Freihof hadn't stopped Mrs. McConnachie when he had, the damage would've grown exponentially greater every second.

Kendrick assured her that every law-enforcement officer in Arizona was looking for Freihof even as they spoke. Somehow that didn't reassure her. But she wouldn't let it worry her right now. Right now she was focused on Brandon.

He had *fought* for her.

Andrea had realized, of course, when he had been teaching her the self-defense moves, that Brandon knew how to handle himself. He was a trained agent, so he would know hand-to-hand combat moves.

This had been more than that.

When Freihof put that explosive necklace around her neck, Andrea had not believed there was any way Brandon would be able to fight and beat someone with the size and cunning of Freihof—who had a *knife*—in three minutes. Some things were just not possible.

She'd watched as Brandon had turned into something else before her eyes. In one second a myriad of conflicting emotions had radiated from him: concern, anger, worry, pain. He'd been thinking of multiple different angles and scenarios to tip the situation in his favor, his powerful mind working in overdrive.

In the second Freihof had turned on the explosives countdown, Brandon's powerful mind had been completely shut down. Every emotion he'd been projecting had stopped. Focus and determination had taken its place.

The intellectual genius had been replaced by a dark warrior. And the dark warrior had achieved the impossible: defeating Freihof before the time had run out.

He had *fought* for her. No one in her life had ever fought for her.

Andrea held Brandon's hand as he slept. Soon his family would be here and she'd be relegated to the waiting room. But for now he was hers to protect.

BRANDON'S BRAIN WOKE UP before he could force his eyes open. That happened a lot. He was processing before he was fully awake.

But for some reason he seemed to be processing more slowly than usual. Frustrating. He forced himself to relax, not opening his eyes. To listen, to remember, to piece it all together.

His first awareness was of the pain. It seemed to radiate from everywhere in his body. Everything hurt so much he couldn't seem to figure out where his central injuries had occurred.

He heard the beeping of machines, distant talking farther away. He was in a hospital. The fight with Freihof, the knife, the explosion... It all came back to him.

"College just wasn't for me," a deep voice was saying. "I had better things to do with my time. Things that provided a much more rounded education, if you know what I mean."

Joe Matarazzo. Brandon knew his friend and fellow agent's voice.

Brandon tried to open his eyes but it was more difficult than he'd thought. The pain wanted to pull him back under.

"You're bad." It was Andrea's sweet voice, but different. More throaty. Hoarse, but damn if it didn't still sound sexy to him. He could feel his hand resting in hers.

"My friends say I'm audacious." Brandon could hear the smile in Joe's voice. "I had to look that up to see what it meant, because of the lack of college education and all. Ends up that 'coming from a billionaire family and sleeping with every available woman in a three-state area' is actually the very definition of *audacious*."

Andrea laughed. "Yeah, well, I'm a high school drop-out ex-stripper. I think that might one-up you."

Had Andrea just made a joke about her past?

Joe's bark of laughter was friendly and kind. "Well, then you and I probably ought to run off and get married right now."

Now Brandon opened his eyes.

"Nope, she's taken." He raised their linked hands.

Joe smiled. "Hey, bro. You gave us a scare for a minute."

Joe said some other things, but Brandon only had eyes for Andrea. She was here. She was safe. She was at his side.

Joe cleared his throat. "I can see that you and your lady need some time, so I'll be back in a while."

Joe made his way out the door. Brandon appreciated the other man's tact.

"Hey," Andrea whispered, leaning over him so she was a little closer.

It cost him considerable effort, but Brandon reached up to bring her lips down to his. He couldn't go another second without feeling her sweetness against him.

"Are you okay?" he asked against her mouth.

"Yes. You were the one who was hurt, fighting Freihof."

"Your voice sounds different."

"That was actually Mrs. McConnachie's doing. Freihof saved me from her so he could kill me himself." He felt her shudder. "But the doctors think my voice should fully recover. And there is no permanent damage. You, on the other hand… Multiple stab wounds, concussion, dislocated shoulder. You're very lucky, all things considered. One of the stab wounds missed your kidney by a couple of centimeters."

"But you're okay." That was all Brandon could remember about his fight with Freihof. The knowledge that if he failed, Andrea would suffer. He couldn't allow that to happen.

She kissed him again. "I'm perfectly fine."

Thank God. He hadn't allowed it to happen.

"But Freihof got away. Kendrick assures me they have a statewide manhunt going for him."

Brandon's teeth ground. As long as Freihof was free Andrea wouldn't be safe. "Does Steve know?"

"Yes. I think that's why Joe is here. He said he was just passing through on another case, but I think Steve sent him to keep an eye on us in case Freihof came back."

Brandon nodded. "We'll get him, sweetheart. I promise."

Andrea smiled. "I know."

"I heard you make a joke about being a stripper with Joe. That took a lot of guts."

Andrea gave him a shy smile. "Given his past, mine didn't seem so bad. Plus, Joe's easy to talk to. He makes everything seem okay somehow."

"That's why he is so good at his job as a hostage negotiator. Everybody loves to be around him."

"Well, I just love to be around you," she whispered.

"Good, because I don't plan on letting you out of my sight."

Her past didn't make any difference to him except

in how it had formed her into the beautiful, intelligent, gutsy woman she was. All Brandon cared about was their future.

A nurse entered the room. "Mr. Han, your family is here."

"Okay, you can let them in."

Andrea stood up. "I'll go wait in the waiting room or find Joe."

Brandon didn't let go of her hand even for a second. "No. Like the nurse said, my family is here." He pulled her down for a kiss. "That includes you, sweetheart. From now on."

Her soft smile balanced out the darkness inside him and appeased the warrior inside.

She was his.

* * * * *

Look for more books in Janie Crouch's
OMEGA SECTOR: CRITICAL RESPONSE
*miniseries later this year. You'll find them wherever
Harlequin Intrigue books are sold!*

SPECIAL EXCERPT FROM

⒣ HARLEQUIN®

I N T R I G U E

*A Texas sheriff gets the surprise of his life when his
ex-wife returns to Appaloosa Pass Ranch claiming her
death was the only way to protect him and their son
from a serial killer.*

*Read on for a sneak preview of
SIX-GUN SHOWDOWN,
the next book in* USA TODAY *bestselling author
Delores Fossen's gripping miniseries
APPALOOSA PASS RANCH.*

"Paige?" Jax whispered.

He could have sworn everything stopped. His heartbeat.
His breath. Maybe even time. But that standstill didn't
last.

Because the person stepped out, not enough for him to
fully see her, but Jax knew it was a woman.

"You got my message," she said. "I'm so sorry."

Paige. It was her. In the flesh.

Jax had a thousand emotions hit him at once. Relief.
Mercy, there was a ton of relief, but it didn't last but a
second or two before the other emotions took over: shock,
disbelief and, yeah, anger.

Lots and lots of anger.

"Why?" he managed to say, though he wasn't sure
how he could even speak with his throat clamped shut.

Paige cleared her throat, too. "Because it was
necessary."

As answers went, it sucked, and he let her know that with the scowl he aimed at her. "Why?" he repeated.

She stepped from the shadows but didn't come closer to him. Still, it was close enough for him to confirm what he already knew.

This was Paige.

She was back from the grave. Or else back from a lie that she'd apparently let him believe.

For a *dead* woman, she didn't look bad, but she had changed. No more blond hair. It was dark brown now and cut short and choppy. She'd also lost some of those curves that'd always caught his eye and every other man's in town.

"I know you have a thousand questions," she said, rubbing her hands along the outside legs of her jeans. She also glanced around. Behind him.

Behind her.

"Just one question. Why the hell did you let me believe you were dead?"

Don't miss SIX-GUN SHOWDOWN
by USA TODAY *bestselling author Delores Fossen,*
available in August 2016 wherever
Harlequin® Intrigue books and ebooks are sold.

www.Harlequin.com

HIEXP0716

Reading Has Its Rewards

Earn **FREE BOOKS!**

Register at **Harlequin My Rewards** and submit your Harlequin purchases from wherever you shop to earn points for free books and other exclusive rewards.

Plus submit your purchases from now till May 30th for a chance to win a $500 Visa Card*.

Visit **HarlequinMyRewards.com** today

MYR16R1

HARLEQUIN®

A Romance FOR EVERY MOOD™

Love the Harlequin book you just read?

Your opinion matters.

Review this book on your favorite
book site, review site, blog or your own
social media properties and share
your opinion with other readers!